ERICA'S COME TO STAY!

"I didn't want to interrupt your meeting, girls," Mrs. Quindlen said, "but the plans changed, so Erica's come to stay with us, starting tonight."

"Tonight?" Stevie said before Meg clamped a hand over her mouth.

Molly barely heard what her mother had said. All she knew was that Erica Soames in her black leggings and brightly colored ski jacket was standing on Molly's own fluffy white rug and breathing the very same air the Friends 4-Ever were breathing. Molly wished she knew *what* was going through her mother's mind.

P.S. We'll Miss You
Yours 'Til the Meatball Bounces
2 Sweet 2 B 4-Gotten
Remember Me, When This You See
Sealed with a Hug
Friends 'Til the Ocean Waves
Friends 4-Ever Minus 1
Mysteriously Yours
C U When the Snow Falls

C U WHEN THE SNOW FALLS

Deirdre Corey

AN
APPLE
PAPERBACK

SCHOLASTIC INC.
New York Toronto London Auckland Sydney

ISBN 0-590-45109-X

Copyright © 1991 by Fastback Press, Inc. All rights reserved. Published by Scholastic Inc. APPLE PAPERBACKS is a registered trademark of Scholastic Inc. FRIENDS 4-EVER is a trademark of Scholastic Inc.

12 11 10 9 8 7 6 5 4 3 2 1   1 2 3 4 5 6/9

Printed in the U.S.A.   40

First Scholastic printing, November 1991

To Deirdre Colligan

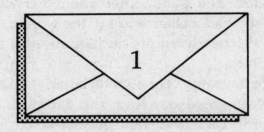

NO VACANCY

Molly Quindlen could feel the hot spotlight warm her face. A circle of light followed her as she tiptoed across the darkened stage. Though the stage was bare, she stepped around an invisible table and walked over to an invisible fireplace.

"Our stockings," she said in a stage whisper. "They're filled."

Molly seemed to lift something down. "Look, Mary," she said to her friend, Meg Milano, who had stepped into the spotlight. "We have our very own tin cups!"

Just the way they had rehearsed a dozen times

in Molly's bedroom, Meg broke into a dimpled smile and pretended to pick up the imaginary cup.

Molly didn't need to check her script for the next lines. She had written them herself. But before she had a chance to say the words, someone in the nearly empty auditorium said something first.

" 'We have our very own tin cups!' " a Donald Duck voice cried out from the darkness. "Just think of it, tin cups," the squeaky voice added.

At that, the spotlight that had been shining on Molly's head zigzagged all over the auditorium and searched for the person who had ruined Molly's special moment. Finally the bouncing light landed on another girl, who ducked before anyone could see who she was.

"Aha!" Molly's friend, Stevie Ames, called out. Stevie was operating one of the spotlights up on the catwalk overlooking the Crispin Landing Elementary School auditorium stage. "Caught ya!"

Molly's big brown eyes followed the beam with horror. There, in the spotlight, were two heads, crouching behind a row of seats. From the stage, Molly could see Mrs. Higgle, the Holiday Concert advisor, march down the aisle. She looked determined to find out who had brought the first rehearsal of "The Little House on the Prairie Christmas" to a halt.

"There they are!" Stevie shouted. Her spotlight lit the backs of the two girls as they crept along row F toward the exit and out the door before Mrs. Higgle could catch them.

Now Mrs. Higgle was in the middle of Stevie's spotlight, and she was vibrating with anger. "I thought I told everyone they were not to bring any friends to the rehearsals. If I said it once, I — "

Molly was too horrified to speak, but Meg sprang to her defense. "Erica Soames and Suzi Taylor are *not* our friends. They wanted to ruin Molly's play!"

Mrs. Higgle pulled on the sleeves of her suit jacket and smoothed back the strands of her dyed black hair. "I beg your pardon. I am quite sure two honor students would not participate in such a prank. Please start all over again, Miss Quindlen, now that your friends have gone."

Molly squinted in Mrs. Higgle's direction. "They're not my friends — " she began before Mrs. Higgle cut her off.

"First line, please."

Again, Molly felt the warm spotlight, only this

time it made her scalp itch. She usually loved being onstage and feeling the darkness around her block out everything but the part she was playing. She tried hard to pretend she was wearing a white flannel nightgown instead of jeans and cowgirl boots, and that she was the young Laura Ingalls Wilder out on the prairie instead of Molly Quindlen playing a part onstage. But her heart was thumping too hard for her to hear the words of the play that had been in her head just a few minutes before the Know-It-Alls wrecked everything. Now she couldn't think of the first word of her own play!

"Miss Quindlen, there are three other numbers to rehearse after yours," Mrs. Higgle's voice shouted out. "Please begin."

Molly opened her mouth, but nothing came out.

"That's it, that's it!" Mrs. Higgle said, waving her clipboard at the stage. "Your rehearsal time is up. It's time for the sword dancers. Sword dancers! Sword dancers, onstage please."

"I just need a minute, Mrs. Higgle," Molly said desperately. "I lost my train of thought."

"I'm afraid you lost more than that. Your group just lost all its rehearsal time as well. Perhaps you might want to consider writing a

4

shorter play or spending a bit more time memorizing your lines *before* you come to rehearsal."

Molly and Meg couldn't get off the stage fast enough for the sword dancers who were whacking away at each other with brown cardboard swords.

Laura Ryder and Shana McCardle rushed in from backstage to comfort Molly. Laura, her long brown hair gathered into an old-fashioned bun to make her look like an 1800's prairie mother, gave Molly a hug. Shana took off the man's cap she'd been wearing and shook it angrily in the direction of the exit door where the girls had escaped without being caught.

Laura could see that Molly was close to tears and put an arm around her. "Never mind, it's just the first rehearsal."

"Yeah," Shana nodded as she put on her parrot earrings now that she wasn't playing the part of Pa Ingalls anymore. "Next time, we'll patrol the aisles and make sure nobody wrecks anything."

Laura stared at the exit door where the girls had disappeared. "I thought Erica and Suzi weren't back from their *Nutcracker* rehearsals in Providence yet. Are you sure it was them, Stevie?"

5

"Of course, it was them," Stevie protested. "Didn't you hear them making fun of Molly's play at lunch yesterday?"

Stevie didn't need to convince Molly. Every chance they'd got in the last week, Erica Soames and Suzie Taylor had made wisecracks about Molly's skit in the Holiday Concert. The quacky Donald Duck voice was just the latest.

Molly pulled her book bag from under one of the aisle seats. "Come on, let's go before I say something to Mrs. Higgle I'll be sorry about."

Molly felt someone pull her back by the belt loop of her jeans. "Don't even think about it, or she'll drop us from the concert," Stevie warned. "You know how horrible Horrible Higgle can be."

Molly sighed. "Do I ever! She didn't even want to include my play at all, but Mrs. Palmer said if the boys could do a robot Christmas skit, Friends 4-Ever could do a prairie one."

Molly's best friends tried not to laugh at the thought of robots dressed up as reindeer and elves, running around the stage. They knew Molly wasn't in the mood for any jokes right then, especially after spending *weeks* writing her short play. She took everything she did very seriously, and it would take a lot more than robot

Santas to make her forget this afternoon.

"Erica and Suzi are just jealous," Stevie said when they went out to the school lobby, "because Mrs. Palmer picked your play instead of letting them dance that scene from the *Nutcracker*. I mean, they're going to dance in it anyway when the New England Ballet comes to school. Hey, what if I put *real* nuts on the stage before their big number and . . ."

Laura ignored Stevie's suggestion for a practical joke. "Honestly, I can't stand that our parents wouldn't let us audition for the New England Ballet *Nutcracker*. I know Molly and I would have made it, I just know it. I swear I'm going to keep my eyes closed the *whole* time Suzi and Erica perform."

"Me, too," Molly said. She felt her cheeks get hot and red at the thought of having to watch Erica and Suzi prance around in beautiful costumes that she and Laura could have been wearing, too. "Well, at least we have my play. That is, if Mrs. Higgle lets us practice and keeps Suzi and Erica out of the way."

Suddenly Molly felt one of Meg's rib jabs. "Ouch! Why did you do that, Meg?"

Meg broke into a big smile and waved to Molly's mother. Mrs. Quindlen was standing next to, of all people, Erica Soames's mother. Through clenched teeth, Meg smiled and talked at the same time. "What's your mother doing with *her*, anyway?"

Molly's wide brown eyes turned into skinny slits. "Ugh," she groaned. "Ever since my mom started working part time at the Board of Education, she's gotten friendly with the Soameses. Would you believe she actually *likes* Erica's mother? I can't stand it."

"Well, you'd better stand it," Stevie said, before heading toward the lobby doors with Shana, Meg, and Laura right behind. "Hi, Mrs. Quindlen," Stevie called across the lobby. "Gotta run!"

Molly grabbed Stevie by her hockey jacket. "Don't leave me here alone, you guys. I'm still so mad about what Erica did, I might be tempted to drop my book bag on Mrs. Soames's foot, and my big, fat history book is in there."

Stevie pulled away. "Sorry, Molly. I don't want to have to curtsy to Erica's mother while I'm wearing my high-tops, so I'm outta here." Stevie winked at her friend. "Save your history book for Erica's foot. Then she can't be the Sugar Plum Fairy or whatever she's gonna be in that dance of hers."

Molly would have laughed at Stevie's idea, but she didn't like the look on her mother's face, the Come-over-and-please-be-polite look.

"Hi, Mom," she mumbled before her mother cleared her throat twice. "Hi, Mrs. Soames."

"Hello, dear," Mrs. Soames said, patting Molly's head as if she were a small dog. "Your mother told me you've been rehearsing a little play you wrote. How sweet! I'm sure it will be delightful."

Molly looked down at her cowgirl boots planted firmly on the floor.

Mrs. Quindlen coughed again, and Molly knew what *that* meant.

"Thank you," Molly finally managed to say.

"My Erica had choreographed a dance to do at the Holiday Concert, but what with being in a *professional* ballet and such, why, there simply wouldn't be time for both. There are endless rehearsals up in Providence, and she'll have to travel all over the state."

Molly could hardly keep from reminding Mrs. Soames that Rhode Island was a very small state, but her mother's own squinty-eyed look kept her from sharing this thought with Erica's mother.

Finally, finally, Mrs. Quindlen came to Molly's

rescue. "Yes, all our girls have such busy schedules. I'm afraid it's my fault Molly didn't try out for the New England Ballet *Nutcracker*. Holidays are so hectic, and there's so much schoolwork, I thought she should wait another year to audition. Maybe next year our girls can try out together."

In no time Mrs. Quindlen and Mrs. Soames went back to talking about whatever boring things they'd been talking about. Molly stood there, wondering how she could pry her mother away and get going downtown where they were *supposed* to start some holiday shopping and not waste time talking to people Molly didn't even like. She got so steamed up listening to her stomach growl for the promised hot chocolate and doughnuts from the Yellow Brick Road restaurant, she almost didn't hear the earthquake her mother nearly caused right there in the Crispin Landing Elementary School lobby.

"That's such a shame. Erica shouldn't have to miss those *Nutcracker* rehearsals while you and Hector are away next week. Maybe she could spend a few days at our house," Mrs. Quindlen was telling Mrs. Soames. "The girls are classmates after all, and we live so close to school. It wouldn't be any problem at all to have her stay with us for a few days."

Molly didn't even try to keep her jaw from dropping.

"Why, Debbie, I really couldn't ask," Mrs. Soames said. "It would be too much of an imposition, but it's lovely of you to offer."

Molly tried desperately to speak in some sort of sign language her mother would understand, but she didn't quite know which combination of frowns, scowls, and hand signals would keep her mother from saying what she said next: "It's no imposition at all, Charlotte, especially since you said the ballet mistress can drive Erica to the rehearsals. Why, when we were out in Kansas, we often had kids in Molly's class boarding with us at one time or another. I kind of miss that custom here in Camden. We just don't get the same chances to be neighborly."

Molly wasn't sure how long she could keep from gagging at the sight of Mrs. Soames's hand patting her mother's arm. "You know, now that you put it that way, I may reconsider, Debbie. This is such a hard time right now, and what with our plans with the Taylors not working out, well, let me talk it over with Erica."

"Talk what over with Erica?" Molly heard next. Fortunately for everyone, Erica Soames wasn't practicing her Donald Duck imitation this time. In fact, she looked at Molly the way she always did, as if she didn't quite know her name.

Mrs. Soames turned to Erica. "Oh, hello, darling. How was your rehearsal up in Providence today?"

"Fine," Erica said. "We just got back this second, and I have to get my makeup work from Mrs. Courtney's office."

Just got back! Molly couldn't get over the smooth way Erica stood there, lying to her mother. She had just gotten back from wrecking Molly's whole afternoon, that's what she'd just gotten back from! What nerve.

"Well, say hello to Mrs. Quindlen, dear," Mrs. Soames said, smoothing Erica's already smooth blonde hair. "Then I'll tell you about the generous suggestion she just made."

"Hi, Mrs. Quindlen," Erica said a little too sweetly for Molly. "What's my mother talking about, anyway?"

Mrs. Quindlen beamed at Erica as if she were a long-lost daughter who had just returned home. "About staying at our house for a few days while your parents are in Boston next week. That way you won't miss your *Nutcracker* rehearsals."

Now it was Erica's turn to make faces. "But, Muuuuther!" she wailed. "You said I could stay at Suzi's. You *promised!*"

Mrs. Soames fidgeted with the collar on Erica's jacket. "It . . . I just found out this morning that Suzi has to stay on at her father's apartment. Her mother won't be back from Chicago by then. Now you know her father only has that tiny apartment. It just won't work out, Erica. Staying at the Quindlens would make a lot more sense. Besides, it would give you and Molly a chance to get to know each other better." Mrs. Soames's voice trailed off when she saw that Erica's face was getting as red as a tomato.

Molly and Erica glared at each other. Molly was fairly sure by the look in Erica's stormy gray eyes that she, too, would rather get to know a rattlesnake.

Molly pulled on her mother's sleeve. "Can we go now, Mom? I have to talk to you."

Somehow Molly managed not to explode in the lobby, but by the time she and her mother got inside the van, she was sputtering like a teakettle on full boil. "Erica Soames? In our house? Eating our food? Using our toothpaste?"

Mrs. Quindlen couldn't help smiling. "Oh, I think she'll bring her own toothpaste," she said as she backed out the van. "What's the problem, honey? Erica's your age, she's in your class, and you've known each other since kindergarten."

"And I haven't liked her since kindergarten, either! She was always the teacher's pet and showing off and not waiting her turn. Just today she ruined my play by imitating me while I was saying my lines during rehearsal. The Friends 4-Ever call her and Suzi the — " Molly stopped just short of telling her mother the name she and her friends had given Erica and Suzi the time when Meg was stuck with them in the Gifted and Special Program. No, her mother would not like hearing Molly call Erica a Know-It-All.

Mrs. Quindlen took a right onto Warburton Avenue. "What *do* the Friends 4-Ever call them?" she asked.

"Nothing," Molly mumbled.

"Nothing? Well, that must be difficult if you have to speak to them and you call them 'Nothing,' " Mrs. Quindlen teased. "Look, we'll straighten this all out. I guess I was a bit quick about offering for Erica to stay with us. But I want you to know there's an important reason I'm helping Mrs. Soames."

"What is it?" Molly asked. What on earth could be so important that Erica Soames had to stay at the Quindlens?

"I can't say right now, Molly," Mrs. Quindlen said in a quiet voice, "but with the holidays and all, I thought we could help them out."

"Why do we have to help out Erica? Besides, I've helped people out for the holidays," Molly complained. "And animals, too." Hadn't she just given up her favorite blanket to bring to the animal shelter now that the weather was so cold? Weren't she and her mother this very afternoon going shopping for something to donate to the toy drive at school? And wasn't Molly the one who suggested that the Friends 4-Ever go caroling at the Camden Nursing Home even though they didn't know all the words to "Winter Wonderland"?

Yes, Molly Quindlen had been a regular Santa Claus lately. So why did she have to be nice to someone who deserved a lump of coal in her stocking?

Of course, Molly couldn't say any of this without turning into Ebenezer Scrooge right there in the van. Instead she began singing a holiday song under her breath with brand-new words:

> *Oh, the weather outside is frightful,*
> *And I'm feeling very spiteful,*
> *If Erica comes, I know,*
> *I will go, I will go, I will go.*

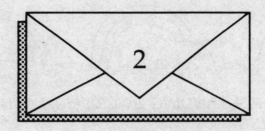

EMERGENCY LANDING

"One, three, five, BOOM!" Molly counted a split second before Stevie burst into her room at seven o'clock that night. "Hi, Stevie," she said without looking up.

"Howdja know it was me?" Stevie said before she crash-landed onto the canopy bed.

"Nobody else makes it up our stairs in four leaps, except for Riggs," Molly answered.

Stevie was wriggling on the bed, trying to pry out a crumpled wad of paper from her jeans. She waved the wrinkled sheet of Molly's rainbow notepaper. "I found your note up in my tree when I went out there to get away from my homework *and* my brothers. Now that I'm here, can you translate it?"

Stevie began reading:

ALIEN LANDING IN CRISPIN LAND-
  ING.
EMERGENCY IFO CREW NEEDED
  TONIGHT.
7:00 MY ROOM.
CU *when night falls and can't get up*

Molly

"What's an 'IFO' anyway?" Stevie wanted to know.

Molly set her wedgie pillow against the wall and plopped back. "An 'IFO,' for your information, is an Identified Flying Object that is about to land in my house. And that's all I can say until Meg and Laura get here."

"We're here because we're here because we're here because we're here," Meg sang in a fake operatic voice when she and Laura popped into Molly's bedroom doorway a few seconds later.

"We're here because we're here because," Laura continued in a quieter voice before she stopped. "Why *are* we here, Molly? I had to tell my mom I needed to borrow an encyclopedia since she wouldn't have let me come out on a school night to check on an alien landing in our neighborhood."

"Aliens, did anyone say aliens?" Meg laughed. She stretched out her springy blonde curls and crossed her blue eyes so she looked like a boingy-haired alien herself. When she finally uncrossed her eyes, she flopped back on the floor mattress the girls used as a couch during their meetings. "Well, I don't actually care why we're here. I finished my history paper, so my parents had to let me out after seeing me suffer for so long. I thought our real meeting wasn't until tomorrow and we were just going to the movies or something. Let's face it, my voice isn't going to get any better by Sunday for our caroling at the nursing home, and since I'm playing Mary Ingalls in your play, even though I wanted to play Laura Ingalls but a certain author wouldn't let me, I only have a few lines and I know them already. And — "

Molly could see Meg was about to take over the whole meeting as she often did. To shut her off, Molly rang a big red sleigh bell she had snitched off the Quindlens' front door wreath. "I wanted you to come over so I could make a big announcement in person. I don't want you to hear this from anyone else at school."

Three pairs of eyes opened wide with worry. "Don't tell us you're moving to Kansas again?" Stevie said. "I don't think I have enough sneaker stationery left for that!"

"Thanks a lot, Stevie?" Molly said. "All you're worrying about is writing letters again? At least Meg and Laura look upset. Anyway, I'll need a lot more than letters for this emergency." She stopped and waited until the only sound in the room was Stevie's gum snapping. "And, believe me, having Erica Soames stay at my house is a true emergency."

Instead of three pairs of worried eyes, now there were three wide open mouths, though

Stevie closed hers before she lost her wad of cinnamon gum.

"Erica Soames is what?" Meg cried when she finally got her jaw working again.

Molly tiptoed over to her bedroom door and shut it quietly. "You won't believe this, I still don't, but my mother actually invited Erica to stay with us next week while her parents are up in Boston. That way she won't miss, get this, the rehearsals for the *Nutcracker* that Laura and I can't even be in, or any of the other neat holiday stuff we're doing at school. Do you believe it?"

This news was just too much for logical Meg Milano, who already had a list of questions about the IFO situation. "Now, just wait a second here. (a) Why can't her parents take her to Boston? Then she can come back with new clothes and a new haircut and brag about it to everybody the way she always does when her parents take her anywhere. (b) Why would the Soameses ask your parents instead of Suzi's? (c) What's the big deal about missing a few rehearsals anyway? (d) — "

"Arrragh!" Stevie said in a strangled voice. "Are you going to go through the whole alphabet, Meg, or are you going to let Molly explain why on earth Erica Soames is going to be staying right in this very house? EEEEW! Just think about it. She'll probably blow a fuse in your house with her hair dryer going nonstop." Though Stevie's wild reddish blonde hair looked nothing like Erica's stylish short hairdo, she flung back her head and flipped her hand across her forehead in a perfect imitation of Erica.

Molly laughed with everyone while they all flung their heads back.

Even quiet Laura got into the Erica Soames act. With her index finger she tried to fluff then smooth her eyebrows the way she'd seen Erica do loads of times. "Gee, Molly. You'll have to build new closets for all the clothes she'll bring since she changes ten times a day. Poor you."

"Maybe you should go to Kansas," Meg said, half seriously. "Anything would be better than having a real, live Know-It-All right in your own house."

Molly leaned back against her pillow. "She's going to ruin everything. We had a zillion things we were going to do together next week, and now I'm supposed to be nice to her. Ugh!"

"Did you tell your mother how she wrecked your rehearsal just this afternoon, never mind the whole rest of *all* our lives with her showing off and bragging all the time?" Meg was determined to solve Molly's problem all by herself.

Molly pretended to read her clipboard. "I tried to tell her, but then she said there's a serious reason why Erica's parents have to go up to Boston."

"Well, what's the reason?" Meg demanded.

"I can't tell," Molly joked, just to get everyone going.

"Can't tell!" Meg, Stevie, and Laura all screamed at once. "Why not?"

"It's much too important," Molly said. She knew this would drive all three girls into a frenzy of curiosity.

Stevie made a werewolf sort of face and stretched her fingertips like claws. "Veee have vays of making you talk," she said in her creepiest Transylvania voice.

The girls started giggling uncontrollably as they tried to tickle the information out of Molly. "Stop it! Oh, no, that's my most ticklish place," she shrieked when Stevie sat on her legs and tickled the soles of her feet.

Molly grabbed her pillow and whomped Stevie over the head. Pretty soon every pillow in the room was flying, along with stuffed bears, rabbits, even Molly's old gray stuffed Babar who didn't look as if he would survive *this* pillow fight.

"Tell us!" Laura shouted as she sent a tattered, stuffed Miss Piggy sailing into Molly's stomach.

"I can't!" Molly shrieked back right before she flung up a small, round pillow that landed like a flying saucer on the canopy of her bed. "My mother wouldn't tell me."

"Sure! Sure!" Meg said.

The girls gasped for breath before lying down on the floor. Stevie made fake threats of launching another attack, but every time she picked up a pillow or stuffed animal, she fell back on Molly's bed and began to laugh.

The girls were laughing so hard, they didn't hear the soft knock at the bedroom door. Nor did they see the door slowly open. Molly was still lying on the floor and holding her stomach when she looked up and saw someone with a big smile and big earrings looking down at her.

She bolted to a sitting position and discovered that, right side up, the big smile was, in fact, a big frown, and it took up most of Erica Soames's face!

What took up most of the hallway were two *giant* duffel bags and a dancer's bag, the very dancer's bag Molly was hoping to get for Christmas. Standing behind all the luggage were Molly's parents.

Mr. Quindlen was ready with a joke before Molly could think of anything to say. "I see you girls are exceeding the fire code again. I'm not even going to try to come inside that sardine can."

Mrs. Quindlen knew better than to joke with Molly. "I didn't want to interrupt your meeting, girls, when Erica's parents dropped her off on their way up to Boston. It was all very last minute, but the plans changed, so Erica's come to stay with us, starting tonight."

"Tonight?" Stevie said before Meg clamped a hand over her mouth.

Molly barely heard what her mother had said. All she knew was that Erica Soames in her black leggings and brightly colored ski jacket was standing on Molly's own fluffy white rug and breathing the very same air the Friends 4-Ever were breathing. Molly wished she knew what was going through her mother's mind. Had the Soames's house burned down? Had Erica's parents decided to disown her all of a sudden? Now *that* was something Molly could definitely understand.

What she couldn't understand at all was the way her mother was acting like a counselor showing a new camper to her cabin. "Why don't you help me get some towels and sheets, Molly, so Erica can settle in? I'm sure the other girls must be getting tired, too. It's a school night, and it's almost bedtime."

"Oh, I don't have a bedtime, Mrs. Quindlen," Stevie blurted out.

Molly's mother didn't miss a beat. "Well, Stevie, we all need our beauty sleep, so let's say good night."

" 'Night, Molly," Meg said, her face twisted into a look of disbelief.

Laura squeezed Molly's hand in sympathy. "See you tomorrow."

"If not sooner," Stevie cracked before she lowered her voice so only Molly could hear her. "I'll leave a ladder outside your window in case you want to run away."

"I'll bring these duffel bags to the guest room," Molly finally managed to say so she could get out of her room before she fainted.

Mrs. Quindlen bit her lip. "I think we'll have to put Erica in here for now, Molly. I've got all the costume materials laid out in the guest room, not to mention some of the gifts I'm sending out to Kansas. Let's find some sheets and blankets and make up the floor mattress in here tonight." Smiling at Erica, Mrs. Soames added, "This is where Molly's friends sleep for sleepovers. I'll get the guest room in shape tomorrow if this doesn't work out."

Molly was pleased not to hear a "Thank you" coming from Erica. She knew her mother wouldn't like that or the way Erica was looking at the sleepover mattress as if someone had asked her to sleep on a bed of nails. Maybe she was going to sleep in the closet, judging from the way she began to shove Molly's clothes to the far end of the closet to make room for her own clothes.

"I'll bet if I stuck a pea under that mattress," Stevie whispered to Molly on her way out, "you'd see her wake up with a backache."

The girls were still too flabbergasted to laugh at Stevie's "Princess and the Pea" joke. When they saw Mrs. Quindlen's disapproving eyebrow go up, they knew it was time to go and headed downstairs.

"Why is she here tonight?" Molly whispered the second she and her mother were safely in the hallway just outside her room. "You said next week, and it wasn't even for sure."

27

Mrs. Quindlen looked more like a tired parent than an enthusiastic camp counselor now. "I'm sorry this happened so suddenly, Molly, but an emergency came up that I can't discuss. I'm very tired right now, so let's try to make the best of it. You would feel differently if you were in her shoes."

Molly did a quick check to make sure Erica couldn't hear her. "You wouldn't let me buy shoes like hers, see." Molly pointed to the bedroom floor where Erica had already unpacked a pair of expensive black leather ankle boots, not to mention jungle print high-tops with black and neon-orange laces.

Mrs. Quindlen did not smile. Instead, she handed Molly some towels. "Now, here, give these to Erica so she can get ready for bed. I know I can trust you, Molly, can't I?"

Molly's mumbled "Yes" came out as if she had pebbles in her mouth.

"Where's the bathroom?" Erica asked when she came out to get her towels.

"It's, uh, it's, uh, it's, uh . . ." Molly finally had to point down the hall since she was still having trouble stringing a sentence together now that the queen of the Know-It-Alls was standing right in her very own house.

Laura and Stevie had been right. Already Erica was in a new outfit, hot-pink nightshirt over a pair of flowered leggings. Molly was just amazed at how someone with just one set of legs could own so many leggings. And, as Stevie had predicted, Erica was carrying a tube of hair stuff, a hair dryer, and what looked like her mother's traveling makeup bag, only much larger.

"I'll come back later to see how you girls are settling in," Mrs. Quindlen said as if tonight were some sort of fun camp-out under the stars.

Erica, on the other hand, seemed to think she was in a hotel. "Oh, do you think I could have one more towel? I want to wash my hair in the morning, so I'll need an extra."

Molly couldn't believe it. How many towels did someone with short hair need, anyway? Erica just helped herself to the biggest towel in the linen closet, her dad's beach towel, which Molly had given him for Father's Day!

Molly could hardly keep herself from picking up the phone to tell her friends the unbelievable things that were happening. But with Erica about to invade her room, Molly decided on a letter instead of a phone call. She grabbed her clipboard and began writing furiously:

Dear Stevie,

If you notice you didn't have any water to brush your teeth with, it's because Erica is using up all the water in Crispin Landing right this minute. Boy, were you ever right. She brought a whole beauty parlor with her.

And guess what no one's noticed! Erica has hardly said one word to me, besides "Where's the bathroom?" Not even "Hi" or "Thanks for letting me invade your life." I'll probably have to bring her breakfast in bed, that is if we have anything in the house that she can eat, because she always says she's allergic to everything. Well, I'm the allergic one right now! And one other thing

Before Molly could get to that one other thing, a shadow fell over her clipboard. A dripping shadow. "Homework?" Erica asked. "Or is that one of those letters you and your little club send to each other like the one Mrs. Higgle captured during study hall last week?"

Molly turned her clipboard facedown on the bed. She could hear different voices wrestling inside her brain. *Try to be nice,* one said. *What nerve!* another voice told her. *Say something back.*

Opening her mouth to speak, Molly had no control over what finally came out: "Your toothbrush is dripping on my bed."

Erica took her wet toothbrush, dried it on the big towel, then let the damp towel slide to the floor. Evidently she had never heard the famous Quindlen warning: "The floor is not a towel rack."

Before Molly could get these words out, her dog, Riggs, came flying into the room. Riggs, a part-Schnauzer, thought clothes on the floor meant tug-of-war time. He grabbed Erica's black leggings, which were also lying on the floor, and raced in circles, hoping someone would chase him.

"Eeeee! What's he doing? Make him stop!" Erica shrieked. "He'll rip my leggings!"

Or maybe your legs, Molly couldn't help thinking. "Riggs! Stop that!" she yelled, diving off her bed to catch the dog.

But Riggs knew this game very well and hid himself under the bed, behind several boxes, stuffed animals, and treasures Molly kept under there. Molly could see Riggs's little coal-black eyes shining with the excitement of the chase. Luckily Riggs's "buddy doll," a mossy-looking brown bear, was down there, too, and Molly finally coaxed him out with that. "Go get it, boy," she said when she tossed the poor eyeless bear into the hall.

Erica rescued her black leggings, which were now covered with dust devils, not to mention some wet teethmarks. "These are ruined!" she said.

"No, they're not," Molly said. "He didn't rip them. He just wanted to play tug-of-war. He always does that when people come to visit."

Erica did one of her famous head flings, and her blonde bangs fell just the way they always did over one eye. With the eye that wasn't hidden by perfect bangs, she glared at Molly. "Well, keep him away from me. I'm allergic to dogs."

"*Sorreee*," Molly said without a smidgen of sympathy. "And by the way, thanks a lot for wrecking my play this afternoon."

There. She'd said it.

Without a flicker of apology, Erica looked at Molly. "What *are* you talking about?"

"You know," Molly said in the deepest, darkest voice she could muster. "You know."

Erica threw down her leggings. "I don't know what you mean. Look, I didn't want to come here any more than you wanted to have me, but you don't have to go around making up stories about me just because your little play isn't working out. Now, tell me. Is there a phone around, or should I go find a pay phone?"

"On that bookcase," Molly answered. Thank goodness she actually had her own phone even though it had taken a year of asking, when she was out in Kansas, to get it. "You can bring it out in the hall." *Too bad the cord's not long enough to stretch to Jupiter where you came from.*

Erica didn't go to Jupiter, but she did carry the phone as far out into the hall as she could without actually pulling it out of the phone jack. She made a big show of closing the door, but even so, Molly heard her say: "Hi, Suzi. It's me. You won't believe where I'm calling from . . ."

Picking up her rainbow pen, Molly had a few words to say herself. She flipped over her clip-

board and added something to the note she had
begun to Stevie:

> And one other thing. I'll need that ladder
> after all.
>
> Yours 'til the Jelly Rolls,
>
> *Molly*

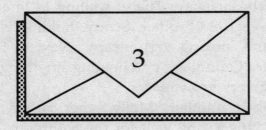

3

HARD TO BE NICE

Whooosh. Whooosh. Whooosh. The sound of the jungle waterfall was soothing as it fell in a silver curtain hundreds of feet from a cliff. Molly stretched out her leg to feel its coolness.

Instead her foot hit a wall, not a waterfall, and she woke up instantly.

"Ouch!" Molly grabbed her foot and held it tight to stop the throbbing. She was still in a jungle all right, a jungle of sheets, blankets, towels, and clothes lying in tangled piles all over her room.

"Mmm, it must be raining outside," she said as the whooshing sound of water continued.

But, no, skinny lines of sunshine squeezed through the sides of the window shades. It wasn't raining outside, Molly realized, but *inside*! She threw back her covers and made her way out to the hallway. There, waiting in line, was her six-year-old brother, Scotty, holding Floppy Dog, and looking very sleepy. Next to Scotty was Mr. Quindlen, not holding anything, but looking very grouchy.

"Grab a number, Molly," her father whispered. "It's a long wait for the bathroom."

"What's taking Mom so long?" Molly asked. "She's usually downstairs by now, isn't she?"

"Mommy's not in there," Scotty said. "That girl is."

So all that whooshing wasn't a waterfall but Erica Soames trying to set a record for the world's longest shower. "How long has she been in the bathroom?" Molly asked her father.

"Since 1872," Mr. Quindlen answered. "You can use the downstairs bathroom, unless you're planning to shave and your razor is in this bathroom like mine is."

"Now, now," Mrs. Quindlen said when she came out of the bedroom to check on why everyone was gathered in the hallway.

Before Molly had a chance to wonder why

her mother wasn't dressed already, everybody jumped a foot. *"Weeeoooo! Weeeoooo! Weeeoooo!"* An unbelievable wail was coming from the hallway smoke alarm.

Scotty raced to his room and stuck his head under two pillows. Molly clamped her hands over her ears, but that barely helped. Meanwhile, her parents stumbled from room to room, trying to find a chair so they could reach the alarm and turn it off.

Finally, Mr. Quindlen brought a chair from their bedroom, climbed up, and ripped out the battery. The horrible noise finally stopped. Mrs. Quindlen sniffed the air several times. "I don't smell any smoke. What made this thing go off, I wonder?"

"Three hours of steam coming from the shower," Mr. Quindlen muttered. "I guess I'll just have to go to work with a beard today."

"Shh," Mrs. Quindlen said, "she might hear you."

"She didn't even hear the smoke alarm, Debbie. How could she hear with the water running like Niagara Falls?" Mr. Quindlen asked. "Look, I'm sorry," he apologized when he saw how pale and tired Mrs. Quindlen seemed even though she'd slept much later than usual. "I know I said

I'd take care of the kids so you could get some extra sleep. Why don't you go back to bed?"

Mrs. Quindlen reached into the pocket of her robe and pulled out a tissue to blow her nose. "Never mind. I'm awake now," she said between sniffles. Just then the sound of the shower finally stopped. "Erica, is everything okay in there?" Mrs. Quindlen called through the door.

"Fine, Mrs. Quindlen," Erica answered, "but I forgot my towel in Molly's room. Can you get it for me?"

"I'll send Molly in. We'll have breakfast soon, so just come right down when you're ready, okay?" Mrs. Quindlen answered. Turning to Molly, she said, "Can you get her that towel she left in your room? My eyes are open, but the rest of my body is screaming for more sleep."

Trudging to her room, Molly grumbled, "What am I, her maid?" Already Erica Soames was even making her mother sick!

"My favorite towel!" Mr. Quindlen said in mock horror when Molly came back. "You let her have my favorite beach towel?"

"You can have my Snoopy towel, Daddy," Scotty said. "She didn't take that one. I'm gonna hide it."

"That's okay, buddy. Now let's go downstairs,

or we'll all be late today," Mr. Quindlen told Scotty.

After everyone was gone, Molly tapped on the bathroom door.

"Come in," Erica sang out.

When Molly opened the door, a warm cloud of steam rushed out. "Here." Molly tossed a very pink-looking, towel-wrapped Erica yet another towel.

Erica expertly wrapped it around her head turban-style. Picking one of a half dozen bottles she had lined up on the sink, she took a tall, skinny, white one and unscrewed the cap. "Lotion," she told Molly while she slathered the stuff over her legs and arms. "I have sensitive skin."

Molly, who hated anything sticky touching her, couldn't believe anyone would actually put on such goo without a mother standing over her with a stick. "You're putting suntan lotion on in December?" she asked.

Erica rolled her eyes. "It's moisturizer, hypo-allergenic."

"Hypo what?" Molly began but changed her mind. She was not going to stand around talking to someone who showered, shampooed, and gooped herself up when she didn't even need to. "Can I get in here pretty soon? I'm going to be late for school if I don't get ready."

Erica made a pickle face while she recapped her hypoallergenic whatever-it-was and shoved all her little bottles into the big makeup bag.

"Excuse me," Molly said, looking on. "I think you put our toothpaste in there."

Erica reached in and fished out the tube. "Sorry. Anyway, I only use tooth gel, not paste." With that, she and her towels walked out the door.

Molly turned on the bathroom fan to clear out the steam and shut the door. She splashed water on her face and brushed her teeth in two quick passes. Finally, she took practically the only towel Erica hadn't used and wiped off the foggy mirror. Then she quickly combed her chin-length hair.

She was done.

Startled, Erica jumped when Molly came into the bedroom. Evidently she didn't realize it was possible for someone to get ready for school in less than an hour.

"Hey, what are you doing?" Molly said when she caught Erica fishing around in her precious 'N Stuff box. Of all the things, nobody was supposed to touch, it was the 'N Stuff box. Her whole world was in there — Friends 4-Ever letters she had received during her long time away in Kansas, a memory book of wonderful experiences with Stevie, Meg, and Laura, and friendship bracelets they had made for each other. Buried under everything, there was even a piece of pavement from Crispin Landing and a lucky rock from Stevie that she had carried around in her pocket for over a year.

"What would I want with this ratty old box, anyway?" Erica said. "I thought my diamond stud fell inside there, that's all. But it was here the whole time."

Molly noticed Erica's hands were shaking as she pushed her diamond stud, a diamond speck really, through her pierced ear. Not to be outdone, Molly checked her own earlobes to make sure her little horseshoe earrings were in place. They were more valuable to her than any old diamonds.

"When you go downstairs, can you tell my mom I'll be down in a couple of minutes?" Molly asked Erica. She was going to check her 'N Stuff box to see if anything had been disturbed.

"I'm not going down yet," Erica answered. "I'm not ready. I still have to dry my hair."

Molly's stomach was rumbling, but she wasn't about to leave Erica alone in her room with her

'N Stuff box or anything else. "We'd better go downstairs, or we won't have time for any breakfast," Molly shouted over the roar of the hair dryer.

Erica was too busy blowing her hair first in one direction then in the other to answer Molly right away. When she did, she didn't even bother to turn off the dryer. "Tell your mom I'll just have juice," she yelled with her head upside down. "Apple. My stomach bothers me in the morning, so I never eat breakfast."

"There's a mirror over there by the bookcase, on the other side of the room," Molly shouted back. She moved Erica's other hairbrushes and the makeup bag from the dresser.

"Fine," Erica answered, snapping off her hair dryer at last. "Maybe your mother will have the guest room ready tonight."

"Or maybe Riggs's doghouse," Molly muttered under her breath as she went downstairs.

"Where's Erica?" Mr. Quindlen asked when Molly came into the kitchen alone. "Not taking another shower, I hope?"

"She said to tell you her stomach bothers her, so she never eats breakfast," Molly answered.

A small frown of annoyance passed over Mrs. Quindlen's face before it changed to concern.

"She's probably homesick, poor thing."

And I'm sick of having her in our home, Molly nearly said until she noticed how her mother was just standing near the counter holding a pitcher of orange juice but not pouring any of it. Molly felt a small flip-flop in her empty stomach. Why was her mother still in her bathrobe, especially with a guest in the house? She didn't know why, but she just didn't want Erica to see her mother in that robe. What if Erica went blabbing to Suzi Taylor and some of the other Know-It-Alls they hung around with about how the Quindlens ran around in pajamas all the time?

Mr. Quindlen looked worried and took over the juice pouring.

"Debbie, you go back to bed, and I'll take care of things down here," he said.

"Can't," Mrs. Quindlen mumbled tiredly. "I want to make sure Molly's friend gets off to school. Ooo, if only my muscles didn't ache so."

"You must be coming down with flu or something," Mr. Quindlen said. "Always happens every year around this time. Now go back to bed. I'll make sure no smoke alarms go off again!" he joked, but no one laughed.

Mrs. Quindlen shuffled out of the kitchen, too tired to give Scotty and Molly the usual reminders about books, boots, and backpacks.

"What's the matter with Mommy?" Scotty asked when he held out his plastic Snoopy cup for some juice. "Can she bring me ice-skating?"

Molly was wondering the same thing but didn't say it. She hated the feeling she always got when her mother got sick. It didn't happen often, but when it did Molly knew she was supposed to act very grown-up and make her own toast and get her own books and not complain about things.

Not complaining. Boy, was that ever hard now!

"Don't worry, guys. I'll get you to skating sometime this week," Mr. Quindlen said. "It seems like Mom's getting some kind of bug."

"Bug! Eee! Is there a bug in the kitchen?" Erica shrieked from the doorway.

"No, there isn't a bug!" Molly said in disgust. "My father meant my mother might have a flu virus or something."

Erica stepped into the kitchen slowly as if she expected to be attacked by giant cockroaches. "Well, I hope she's not contagious. I have my *Nutcracker* rehearsals and performances for the next two weeks, and I know Miss Sophia

44

wouldn't want my understudy to take my part. I'm the Sugar Plum Fairy, you know."

"So I heard," Molly muttered. At least seventy-two times!

Unlike Molly, Mr. Quindlen tried to act impressed. "Big part, huh? Well, the rest of us are healthy, so I wouldn't worry about getting sick in this house. Here, have some orange juice."

"Erica doesn't drink orange — " Molly began, but Erica had already pushed the juice glass away from her place at the table.

"If you have all-natural apple juice, I'll take that," Erica said in a syrupy voice.

Molly saw her dad make a funny face when Erica wasn't looking. He checked the depths of the refrigerator then went over to the sink and ran water into a glass. "Sorry, guess you'll have to settle for some all-natural tap water," he said.

"Dad!" Molly protested before her father could think of any more embarrassing comments.

"Just kidding," Mr. Quindlen said, but Molly knew he wasn't kidding at all. The whole family knew how Mr. Quindlen felt about picky eaters, not to mention people who hogged the bathroom.

Molly sank into her chair. She could already hear Erica blabbing to Suzi Taylor that the

Quindlens served their houseguest water instead of juice.

"If you have some bottled water, that would be fine, Mr. Quindlen," Erica said. "See, I think I'm allergic to — "

"Um, I just remembered. I have to get my homework," Molly broke in before her father offered Erica a dry bread crust. She had to tell someone about her incredible morning before she burst. Her friends just wouldn't believe it.

Molly raced upstairs, shut the door to her room, and grabbed the phone. Picking up the receiver, she was about to press the first button of Stevie's number when she heard someone on another extension. Was Erica hogging the phone again? It wasn't even eight o'clock yet!

Molly listened. "Yes," she heard her mother telling someone. "Well, I wish I didn't have to come in so soon after the last visit with Dr. McDade, but I'm afraid I'm not feeling well again. Do you have any appointments today?"

Now Molly felt kind of woozy and tried to set the phone down so her mother wouldn't hear her nervous breathing on the extension. Her mother *never* went to the doctor, and now she was saying she had just been there and needed to go back again.

What kind of a "bug" did her mother have, Molly wondered. The Erica Soames Flu?

Molly tiptoed to the hallway and put her ear next to her parents' bedroom door. Her mother was still on the phone, and Molly could only make out a few snatches of what her mother was saying, something about blood tests and a "CAT scan," whatever that was, then something about an operation.

Molly felt something heavy, something like a brick, land on her heart. She'd had that brick-on-the-heart feeling before — when Grandma Quindlen died; when they gave her cat, Marmalade, away because of Scotty's allergies; and of course, when she left her friends behind to go to Kansas. Was something bad happening again?

She walked back to her room to wait for her mother to hang up.

"Will you be done with your call soon?" Erica said when she came upstairs and found Molly holding the phone in her lap.

"What? What?" Molly said, lost in her gloomy thoughts.

"Will you . . . ? Never mind," Erica said in a loud huffy voice. "We have two phone lines at our house, so there's always one free."

Before Molly could think of something to say back, she heard her mother call out from the bedroom. "Erica! Erica! I have your mother on the phone. You can pick it up in Molly's room."

Erica leaped over her two duffel bags to get at the phone. "It's my mother."

Molly didn't move.

"It's my mother!" Erica repeated, loudly this time. "I want to talk to my mother pri-vate-ly. Get it?"

Molly got it and handed the phone over before slamming the door behind her so Erica could talk "pri-vate-ly."

She tapped on her mother's door. No answer. She pushed the door open and hoped that when she went into her parents' room, everything would turn out to be normal after all. Her mother would be pulling on the red-and-white snow-flake sweater she often wore around the holi-days. She would have a list of chores for everyone in the family to do. She would remind Molly to bring the newspapers to the curb be-cause it was recycling day.

But there was no busy mother inside, no snowflake sweater, or list of chores to hear about. The room was gray and dim, and Mrs. Quindlen didn't stir, not even when Molly stepped on the squeaky floor board on purpose. That usually woke her mother up even if it was three o'clock in the morning and Molly was having a bad dream.

"Mom?" Molly called softly. "Mom?"

Her mother didn't move. Molly moved the phone off the bed to the night table in case her mother rolled over. She walked out of the room and stepped on the squeaky board again. It made no difference. Her mother was still asleep.

Molly poked her head into her bedroom where Erica was still talking on the phone. "Can you lower your voice? My mother is *trying* to sleep."

In answer, Erica pushed the door shut on Molly. She felt all alone now, and the heaviness pressed harder on her heart. Her mother wasn't *trying* to sleep at all. For some reason, her mother couldn't *help* sleeping.

RUNAWAY FEELINGS

The music blaring from the loudspeaker was scratchy, and the words to the songs vanished into the cold night air without being heard. But Molly didn't care. And she didn't care that, as usual, the Camden Parks Department had plowed off more ice for hockey than for the slow skating she liked to do. At last she was about to have some fun after being cooped up for two days at home helping out, because her mother was still sick and because they had a Know-It-All houseguest who didn't seem to know how to clean the bathroom, bring a dish to the sink, or put a towel in the hamper.

After two days of chores, chores, and more chores, Molly enjoyed the sight of the winter sky dusted with a million stars and Patriot's Pond fringed with the holiday lights of nearby houses. Being out at nighttime, with no parents and no little brother, made her feel just like some of the older kids she saw skating around or gathered in groups here and there. As she laced up her skates, she felt sure they would take her flying across the pond, and she would suddenly be able to skate backwards, do spinning turns, and flying leaps.

Off at the far end, Molly could see Stevie zooming around with the hockey skaters, trying to sweep a dot of a hockey puck into the net. At the near edge of the pond Meg and Laura were skating backwards but not getting very far. And hogging the middle of the ice was a group Molly tried not to notice, the Know-It-Alls, Erica and Suzi, and a bunch of older kids she didn't know.

"Honestly, they look like a bunch of penguins trying to keep warm," Meg said when Molly skated up.

Right then Stevie whizzed up and very nearly knocked everyone down like bowling pins. "Come on," she said, all out of breath. "Are you guys going to skate or just stand around talking like *them*? Would you believe that the greatest hockey skater in Camden, next to me that is, my very own blood brother, Mike Ames, is over there with *them*, and not skating? I'd like to sneak over and tie his laces together. What a waste of perfect ice!"

Boys. That's what Molly, Stevie, Meg, and Laura tried not to notice hanging around with the Know-It-Alls.

"Mike's probably just hanging out with Sean Taylor, Suzi's brother," Laura said to make Stevie feel better.

"Yeah, right," Stevie grumbled, kicking at the ice with the point of her right skate. "I'm never going to middle school if that's what happens to people."

Molly tried to skate and think at the same time. Yes, this hanging around with boys definitely did seem to be something that "happened to people," and, by the looks of things, it was already happening to Suzi and Erica.

"I don't know why they bring skates at all," Meg said in disgust. "They just stand in the middle of the ice like some kind of island that we have to skate around. Honestly!"

"I'll get them to move," Stevie shrieked, and she was off in a blur of flying hair and churning arms. She whizzed up to the group but stopped just short of plowing into it. Nobody looked up.

"They didn't even notice you," Molly said, a little embarrassed by Stevie's antics.

"They will when I take a saw and cut a hole around them!" Stevie joked before streaking off again.

Molly, Laura, and Meg threaded arms and slowly glided off, careful to support each other so they wouldn't take an embarrassing spill in front of everyone.

"I didn't think you'd get out tonight," Laura said to Molly. "I'm sure glad you did."

"Thanks, Laura. I was going to run away from home if my parents didn't let me come skating," Molly explained. "Erica's been out the last two nights with her rehearsals *and* skating, while I've had to do the dishes and clean the bathroom and help Scotty with his homework *and* bring stuff to my mom."

"I hate when my mom gets sick. Thank goodness she hardly ever does," Meg said. "I mean, that's when I hate being an only child. I feel as if I should make her chicken soup or something, but I certainly can't cook anything!"

"Me, neither!" Laura said. "And I'm never going to cook."

"I agree," Meg said. "When we have our own apartment, we can just eat peanut butter sandwiches."

"Or pizza from La Piazza," Laura added. "I'd have that every day. What about you, Molly?"

"Earth to Molly, Earth to Molly," Meg said.

Molly didn't want to think about her mother being at home in bed for the third day straight, but talking about sick moms made her forget for a minute that she was supposed to be having fun.

"Something wrong, Molly? Besides having Erica living in your house, I mean?" Laura asked, her voice full of concern.

"Not that that isn't a reason for looking mopey," Meg said. "I'd sure be depressed if I had to be in the same house with *her*," she added. She stared across the pond. Now she could see Erica and Suzi doing some spins as if they were stars in the Ice Capades.

Meg put her hands on her hips. "Well, if we had *thousands* of ice-skating lessons we could do that, too."

"Come on, let's go back to the rock," Laura suggested to get away from the Erica Soames Ice Show and find out what was bothering Molly. "I told my mom I didn't want to drag around a thermos of hot chocolate, but we might as well have it."

Meg waved Stevie over, and all four girls made their way up a small hill to "their" spying rock where they could see all the skaters but no one could see them. Laura passed some plastic cups around, and the girls took big drinks of the steaming hot chocolate.

"When are her parents coming back, anyway?" Meg asked.

"Whose?" Molly answered as she stared off into space.

"Erica's, silly," Meg said. "I thought that's why you got so serious all of a sudden, when you saw her buzzing around like a queen bee over there. I'd sure be depressed if I was going home in a little while and she was going to be there, too.

Molly sniffled. "That's only part of it."

"I hope you don't have to serve her breakfast in bed, do you?" Stevie asked. " 'I'll have some buttered scones, or perhaps some crumpets, and of course some fresh-squeezed orange juice, that is, after you make my bed then call my chauffeur to bring me to school.' "

"Stevie!" Laura scolded. "Can't you see Molly doesn't feel like fooling around?"

Molly swirled the last of her cocoa in her cup. "It's okay, guys. But it's not Erica I'm worried about, it's my mom. I think she's sick, but not with the flu."

"I thought it was just a cold," Stevie said. "I mean, I know she's in bed and stuff, but she's probably tired from Christmas shopping and buying you tons of stuff, ha-ha!"

Molly shook her head sadly. "It's not just a cold. She's been on the phone to the doctor about getting tests and things," Molly said. "She wouldn't be going to the doctor's for a cold."

Laura poured more cocoa into Molly's cup. "What kind of tests? How did you find out? Why didn't you tell us?"

"Blood tests and maybe an operation," Molly answered. "And something called a CAT scan."

"An X-ray for cats?" Stevie joked before Meg jabbed her in the side. "Sorry, Molly."

Molly poked at the snow with the toe of her skate. How could she tell her friends she'd been eavesdropping on her mother's phone calls and her parents' conversations from outside their bedroom? Or that she'd looked up scary stuff in the medical book her parents kept in the den? Even her close friends might think she was getting weird.

As usual, Laura said the right thing. "You can tell us, Molly. Remember that time I thought we were moving just because my dad wanted to sell our lawnmower at the tag sale? If I'd talked to you guys, you probably would have told me that my dad probably wanted a new lawnmower, not a new house. Maybe it's something like that."

"I don't think so, Laura, but thanks anyway," Molly began. "I overheard my mom talking about medical tests and stuff three times in the last two days. And when I looked up what a CAT scan was in this big medical book we have, it said it's some big test to look for cancer kinds of things. I think that's what my mom's been on the phone about."

"Wow," Stevie breathed. "I hate those kinds of phone calls where they're whispering and you can only hear one side. My mom has lots of those with my dad when they get into fights over the phone. Afterward she tells us it wasn't a fight. Sorry I kidded you, Molly."

"That's okay, Stevie," Molly said. Now all the

happy voices on the pond and the scratchy songs on the loudspeaker seemed to belong to a movie, not something she was part of. Her feet were cold, her nose was starting to run, and her hat was itching her forehead. "You know what? I'm going to wait for my dad in the shed. He'll be here in ten minutes, anyway. Why don't you guys skate, and I'll see you when he gets here."

"No way," Laura said. "I'm coming, too. What about you, Meg? And Stevie?"

Molly pushed Stevie toward the ice. "You stay, Stevie. Erica's supposed to come home with us. Maybe once the queen bee is gone, Mike might start acting like a normal person and play ice hockey with you."

Stevie broke into a big smile and hugged Molly. "You're a real pal, a great buddy, and a — "

"Friend 4-Ever, I know, I know," Molly said, glad that at least Stevie was still having a good time. "Now just don't skate off until I go get Erica. I can't face her alone."

"I don't blame you," Laura said as all four girls skated to the middle of the pond. By the time they reached the group, Erica had finished showing off her spins and was back in the center of the huddle with her friends.

". . . and then I told the guy sitting next to me on the lift, 'I just dropped my ski pole. Do you think I could borrow yours to get off the mountain and then bring it back up on the lift?' "

"Boy, I wish I had a ski pole right now," Stevie muttered.

Molly waited for the hysterical laughter die down. "Erica?" she shouted over the heads of the group. "Erica? It's almost time for our ride."

Everyone kept right on talking and laughing.

Molly saw Stevie form a megaphone with her hands and open her mouth as wide as it would go. "PAGING ERICA SOAMES! ERICA SOAMES! YOUR LIMO IS WAITING IN FRONT OF THE SKATING SHED!"

At that, every head in the group swiveled to see where the shouting was coming from.

"I heard you, I heard you!" Erica said, making her way through the huddle like a celebrity trying to get through a crowd of fans. She turned to her shadow, Suzi Taylor, who was right behind. "It's Molly Quindlen, who else? I practically have to sign in and out of their house whenever I go anyplace."

Molly looked down at the ice to avoid all the annoyed stares aimed in her direction.

"I'm going home with Heather Barbelet," Erica announced. "I told your father that when Suzi's dad picked me up. So you and your friends can run along without me, okay?"

"But, but . . ." Molly tried to explain about there being a nine o'clock curfew at the Quindlens, but she stopped when she saw Erica's friends looking at her like she was someone's pesky little sister breaking up a super party.

Molly's face was burning with embarrassment even before she got to the overheated skating shed where people were warming themselves around a potbellied stove.

"Hey, guys, where are you going in such a hurry?" Molly heard when she swept by Shana and some other girls who were putting on their skates as she was unlacing hers.

Meg put a finger to her lips and pointed to Molly. "Erica got everybody mad because she's supposed to go home with Molly," she whispered to Shana. "But she won't leave."

"What else is new? Erica's such a pain," Shana said sympathetically. "Want me to go out and tell her to get in here?"

"Thanks, Shana," Molly said as she tied her skate laces in a knot that would take *years* to untangle the next time she went skating. "All I know is my dad is going to be real mad when he gets here and finds out she's not coming home with us. You know how my parents are about coming home on time. They would never make me come home at nine and let her stay out later. It wouldn't be fair."

Molly was just getting her boots on when she noticed a familiar pair of men's snow boots planted in front of her.

"What wouldn't be fair?" Mr. Quindlen said with a laugh. "That I'm five minutes early, Molly? Sorry, I could have waited in the van, but I didn't want to turn into a block of ice. Besides, I'm on my way back with some wonton soup for Mom, and I don't want *that* to turn into a block of ice."

"Speaking of blocks of ice," Molly sputtered. "Erica is still skating. She said she didn't have to come home with us and that you and Mom said it was okay. I started to tell her that we had to be home by . . ." Molly stopped. There was something about the way her father was shifting his weight from one boot to the other that she didn't like one bit.

Mr. Quindlen cleared his throat. "About that, Molly. Well maybe we can discuss that when we get home." He nodded toward the other girls.

Molly didn't care if everyone in the skating shed was listening. Snapping on her blade guards, she said: "You mean it's true? She can stay, and I have to go home?"

Mr. Quindlen helped the girls gather up their skates, and gloves, and scarves before he answered. "Hmm, well, I know it looks that way, but there are some . . . some special circumstances we can talk about when we get home."

The girls waved good-bye to Shana, then followed Molly's father out to the parking area. What *was* he talking about?

It was a good thing Mr. Quindlen put on the window defoggers in the van because Molly was steaming. And because she was steaming, Laura and Meg steamed out of sympathy, too, and kept their thank-yous to a minimum when Mr. Quindlen let them off.

"Leave a note in my mail spot," Meg mouthed to Molly when she got out of the van. This looked like one of those times when it wasn't going to be easy to talk on the phone.

When Mr. Quindlen pulled into the driveway at home, Molly slid open the van door, grabbed her skates, and ran into the house, not even feeling the jabs and bumps of her skate blades against her sides. She needed to talk to her mother.

Dropping her skates by the front door, she ran upstairs and knocked on her parents' bedroom door. "Mom! Mom! Can I come in? It's important."

"Oh, I thought you were my wonton soup, Molly," Mrs. Quindlen said as she tried to prop herself up in bed.

At the sight of her mother, Molly forgot all the horrible things she had rehearsed on the ride home. Her mother's short, glossy brown hair, cut just like Molly's, was all flattened on one side and very stringy and lifeless. Instead of a nice nightgown, Mrs. Quindlen was still wearing the old sweatsuit she had put on the day before when she had tried, but failed, to come down for a meal with the family. She didn't look one bit better.

"I'm sorry I'm not your soup," Molly said, biting her lip. "I can go downstairs and get it if you want it now."

Mrs. Quindlen signaled for Molly to come over. "Not right away. Here, sit on the bed, not too close so you don't catch whatever this awful thing is I have. Tell me about skating. Did you have fun?"

"Sort of," Molly answered, pulling at a thread on the quilt.

"Just sort of, Molly? I was hoping tonight would make up for the last few days. You've been such a help with Scotty, and everything that needs doing, not to mention putting up with our houseguest." Mrs. Quindlen patted Molly's cold hands with her too-warm ones. "Did your only 'sort-of-good' time have anything to do with Erica?"

Molly nodded. For once, she was glad that her mother was such a good mind reader.

"If I weren't feeling so under the weather, maybe I would have had a more sensible talk with Mrs. Soames, but I was too tired to argue," Mrs. Quindlen said with a sigh.

"Argue about what?"

Mrs. Quindlen sank back into her pillows tiredly. "Well, I've been trying to imagine how hard it is for Erica's parents to be away without her and have to work things out over the phone. Erica was so upset during her last phone conversation with her parents that she got them to promise she could do certain things."

For a second, Molly pictured Erica running through Razzmatazz's Clothing Store with a giant gold charge card and buying out the store.

Unfortunately, the reality was worse. "Like staying out late tonight?" she asked in a shaky voice.

Now it was Mrs. Quindlen's turn to pull on a piece of quilt thread. "That and some other things. I would have bent the rules for you tonight, too, but I fell asleep before I could tell Dad. Besides I don't think the Milanos or Laura's parents would have liked it."

Well, I didn't like it either, Molly thought without actually saying those words. How could she, when her mother looked so sick and had just finished telling her what a big help she was and everything? She didn't want to disappoint her by losing her temper. "Can I stay in here a little while, Mom?" Molly asked in a gentle voice. She needed her mother more than she needed to be mad.

Mrs. Quindlen smiled. "Okay, I'll pull up a pillow while you get us some of the soup Dad brought home from Happy Gardens. I'm hoping that will cure me."

Molly hoped that would cure her mother, too, not some awful machine in a hospital. "I'll be right back with the tray."

Mr. Quindlen was unloading the soup container from the brown bag when Molly came down. "You two have a good talk?" he asked.

She didn't try to hide her pout. After all, she didn't have to be really nice to her dad. *He* wasn't sick. "Sort of, but it's no fair that Erica got to stay out and I had to come home."

"Nope," Mr. Quindlen agreed. "You're right. It's no fair."

"Well I hope she freezes out there, and they don't find her until spring!" Molly said as she poured the steaming soup into two bowls.

"Then maybe I'd have some hot water to shave with," Mr. Quindlen said with a wink.

Molly turned away so he wouldn't see her tiny smile.

"If my nose weren't so stuffy, I know this would smell delicious," Mrs. Quindlen said when Molly came in. "Channel 9 is showing *National Velvet*. We missed part of it, but since we've seen it so many times already, I don't think it matters."

"Oh, goody! I love that movie," Molly said. She turned on the set just as the heroine's mother was saying: "Things come suitable to the time, Velvet. Enjoy each thing, then forget it and go on to the next."

Molly carefully balanced her bowl and plate on her lap and settled down to watch the movie. The warmth of the noodles and broth and the chance to see one of her all-time favorite movies made everything seem right again.

Maybe nothing serious was wrong with her mother that a little soup from Happy Gardens couldn't fix.

GOOD NIGHT, BAD NIGHT

"Were we the best in the world, Mother?"

"Yes, dear, the best in the world."

Eyes glued to the screen, Molly reached across the bed. "Can I have the tissue box, Mom? The sad part's coming up."

But Mrs. Quindlen didn't answer. She had fallen asleep. And by the looks of the tray by the bed she had fallen asleep without touching her soup.

The wonton soup cure hadn't worked.

The movie wasn't over, but Molly's cozy time with her mother was. She turned off the television just as Velvet Brown was hugging her own mother in happiness.

When Molly came into the kitchen with the tray, her father was talking in an angry voice on the phone. "You mean to say she didn't come home with you? Then who did she go home with? You don't know? Well, never mind."

Molly hoped to get out of the kitchen before her father saw her, so she tiptoed to the counter and put down the tray as quietly as she could. The last thing she wanted to get mixed up in was an argument about Erica Soames.

"Hold it just a sec, Molly," Mr. Quindlen said when he hung up. "I don't suppose you have any idea how Erica was getting home, do you? I just called the Barbelets. They got back from ice skating over an hour ago and didn't even know they were supposed to drive Erica to our house."

"That's what she told me, Dad," Molly answered. "Maybe she went home with Suzi Taylor." Ooo, was Erica ever going to get it now!

Mr. Quindlen flipped through the phone book to the T's and then slapped his forehead. "What's the matter with me? I already called the Taylors and there was no answer. You know, if it wasn't for the fact that the Soameses are going through such a rough time, why I'd — "

"Suzi's at her dad's this week, but he has an unlisted number," Molly told Mr. Quindlen to calm him down. "Erica's got an address book. Maybe the number's listed in there. Should I go see?"

Mr. Quindlen slammed the phone book shut. "Might as well. I don't know who else to call. If she's not at the Taylors I'll go back to the skating pond, then who knows? Just don't wake your mother when you go up. She's got enough to worry about."

"I won't."

When Molly opened the guest room door she couldn't believe how quickly Erica had redecorated the usually tidy little room to look just like a clothing store that had been hit by a tornado. Under a nightshirt and a pair of studded jeans, Molly finally unearthed Erica's backpack. There was a good chance the address book was in there, Molly reasoned, since Erica carried the silvery notebook everywhere as if it contained the private phone numbers of movie stars.

Feeling around in the front pocket of the backpack, Molly pulled out something round and hard. A piece of chewing gum!

"Ugh!" she cried, dropping the disgusting

thing back in the pocket. "What a slob!"

The duffel bag was next. Molly scrabbled through the leggings, sweatshirts, and underwear, but didn't see the address book. Could she have taken it skating? No, Molly decided, even Erica Soames wouldn't bring her address book ice-skating!

Just as Molly was stuffing the last pieces of clothing into the duffel bag, she spied something red and green and spangly — something very-familiar. She couldn't believe it! What were her brand-new reindeer socks doing in Erica's duffel bag?

Molly was clutching the precious socks in her hand when she heard the bells on the front door wreath jingle and felt a draft of cold air follow. Still holding the socks, she ran downstairs where Erica was peeling off her boots and jacket as if she'd just been out for a five-minute stroll around the block.

"Sorry I'm late," Erica sang out to Mr. Quindlen who was staring at her in disbelief. "The Pattersons took me out for hot chocolate after skating."

Molly could see her dad trying hard to keep in mind that Erica was a guest, but he wasn't doing a very good job of it.

71

Erica's voice wasn't quite so chirpy now. "Uh . . . the Pattersons and my parents are friends," she explained. "They said it was okay."

"I — only — wish — you — had — called — to — let — us — know," Mr. Quindlen said slowly, as if he were trying not to explode in anger. "Now, young lady, you'd better get upstairs. I think we'll need to discuss a few house rules in the morning."

Darn. Molly couldn't believe her father was so calm. It wasn't fair. Why, if she was *five minutes* late coming home, her parents took away five minutes from something she liked to do. Meanwhile, Erica Soames could sail in and out of the house whenever she wanted, and all she got was this little talking to!

There was only one thing that gave Molly any satisfaction. That was noticing that she and Erica actually had something in common. Their lower lips trembled right before they started crying!

"When are my parents coming home?" Erica wailed right before she turned on the waterworks.

Molly saw her father roll his eyes helplessly. "Now there, there," he said to quiet down Erica's sobs that were building up in volume. "The main thing is you're home safe and sound."

Erica's rosy cheeks were soon streaked with tears. "But this isn't my home! I want my parents," she said before she raced upstairs and slammed the guest door behind her.

Mr. Quindlen shook his head. "Well, I'll certainly be glad when this is all over, and our house returns to normal. What with mom being sick and Erica's three-hour showers, and the orange juice, and — "

"And her stealing my socks," Molly yelled, shaking the reindeer socks at her confused dad. "I found *my* socks in *her* duffel bag. These are the ones Kristy sent me from Kansas last week for Christmas, and Erica took them. And the other day she was in my 'N Stuff box, and now I can't find some things that were in there."

Both Mr. Quindlen and Molly looked up when they sensed someone listening in. Staring down on them was a teary Erica — a *furious* teary Erica. "I did not go into your stupid box, and those socks you're holding are mine!" she said. "Give them back."

Mr. Quindlen tried to calm the girls, but it was too late. He was too tired and the girls too upset with each other to pay any mind to him.

"I will not give them back!" Molly protested. "My best friend in Kansas sent them to me as a present, and you stole them!"

Erica's gray eyes were dark with anger. "I bet you didn't even check your own room, not that you can find anything in the mess."

"Speaking of mess, at least I don't put old pieces of chewed gum in my backpack!" Molly spit out before she could stop herself.

Erica ran to the guest room. "What were you doing in my backpack and my duffel bag, anyway?" she screamed. "You had no business in there!"

Molly followed right behind her. Erica Soames was not going to win this argument. "I was trying to find that stupid address book you always carry around so my parents could find out whether you were kidnapped or not. But no, you were too busy having fun with the Pattersons to even call to tell them where you were."

At that, Erica slammed the door and started wailing all over again.

Molly was still staring at the closed guest room door when her parents' bedroom door slowly opened. Standing there was Mrs. Quindlen, pale and sicker looking than she had been all week.

"Molly, could you go get Dad?" her mother whispered in a raspy voice that made Molly forget all about Erica Soames.

"Dad! Dad!" Molly called out, and her father was upstairs in a second.

Except for the terrible pounding of her heart, Molly felt as if she were watching a slow-motion movie that she was acting in at the same time.

"Bill," Mrs. Quindlen whispered. "I have a pain in my chest. I think I should go to the emergency room."

Mr. Quindlen's eyes widened in alarm. "I'll call Judy Ames to come over and watch the kids, and then I'll get you to the emergency room."

Emergency room! Molly remembered the awful time she had fallen from a giant snowbank at the end of Half Moon Lane and had had to have her arm X-rayed. During the endless time they'd had to wait for the X-ray person to show up, Molly had seen bleeding people come in from ambulances, people who couldn't breathe and needed plastic masks filled with air right away. Was her mother one of those very sick people?

"Honey, don't look so worried," Mrs. Quindlen said to Molly. "It's probably something called walking pneumonia. Like a bad cold. Not serious," she gasped in a voice that seemed terribly serious to Molly.

"Don't talk, Debbie," Mr. Quindlen said when he got off the phone. "Judy'll be here any minute. The sooner we get you to the emergency room, the sooner we'll be back with some medicine to clear you up so you can get some rest."

A few minutes later Molly heard the rumble of footsteps on the stairs and looked up just in time to see Stevie land with a thud in the hallway. "My mom's right behind me," Stevie announced.

Sure enough, Mrs. Ames came bustling upstairs. "Here's your coat, Debbie, and a blanket to keep warm. The emergency room is always freezing, isn't it, Stevie?"

Stevie, who was wearing a pair of her brother's old G.I. Joe pajamas, nooded. "I should know after all the sports injuries I had to get X-rayed. I'm famous there. You should bring some food, Mrs. Quindlen. They make you wait so long, you'll be starving."

Mr. and Mrs. Quindlen managed a smile, but Molly couldn't believe that her mother could be dying of pneumonia, and Stevie was making wisecracks. "Stevie!"

"Bill, talk to Molly," Mrs. Quindlen whispered hoarsely. "Then we'll go. Judy and I will meet you downstairs."

Mr. Quindlen steered Molly to her room and sat her down on the bed. "Hey, Molly Melinda. Don't look so scared. The only reason we're going to the hospital is because Dr. McDade doesn't have office hours now. He warned Mom she might be developing something called walking pneumonia, but Mom thought she could wait a day to get the medicine. That's all it is, okay?"

Molly nodded, but she didn't believe a word her father was saying. People died of pneumonia and chest pains. Nothing her dad said was going to make her believe anything different.

"You hold down the fort here in case Scotty wakes up. And when our houseguest calms down in there, tell her we'll be right back."

Mr. Quindlen hugged Molly tight, but what she really needed was to hug her mother. She ran downstairs to give her one. " 'Bye, Mom," she said, trying to feel her mother through the fat down coat she was wearing.

"Everything'll be fine," Mrs. Quindlen began before she started coughing so hard she couldn't even say good-bye.

"Here are some quarters for the phone, Bill,"

Mrs. Ames said. "These, a few magazines, and this blanket will make the time go faster. See you in a bit."

Molly stood at the glass storm door and watched the van back out and its taillights disappear down the street. When she turned around, Stevie was right there, hoping she could cheer up her frightened friend.

"Your mom told mine I could sleep over."

"Oh," was the only thing Molly could say to that news.

Usually a surprise sleepover with Stevie would have made Molly jump up and down with excitement. But there was no jumping tonight. Instead she went up to her room quietly, and Stevie followed behind. When they got to the upstairs hallway, the door to Erica's room was open, and Mrs. Ames was just coming out.

"Why don't you girls visit with Erica a bit? She's a little homesick," she whispered. "I'm afraid all the confusion tonight hasn't helped."

Molly was too worried to say anything, but Stevie couldn't keep from blurting out a protest. "But, Mom," she whispered. "Molly's the one that should be upset, not *her*."

Mrs. Ames gave Stevie a warning look that Stevie understood right away. "Oh, all right, but only for a little while. That's all the niceness I've got. Come on, Molly. Let's get it over with."

Not wanting to get Mrs. Ames's warning look, too, Molly tiptoed into the guest room after Stevie. Erica was sitting up on the bed and breaking two Quindlen rules at the same time: no shoes on the bed and no watching television after ten o'clock. She didn't even look up at Stevie and Molly when they came in, and went right on going through the tissue box as if she were determined to empty it before the night was over. In fact, the bed was positively *covered* with crumpled tissues!

Upset as she was, Molly couldn't help noticing how red and blotchy Erica's face was, especially her nose. She didn't look a bit like a Know-It-All now.

"What are you watching?" Stevie asked after an endless amount of time passed by and Erica didn't say anything to the two girls.

"The *Three Stooges*," Erica sniffled. "I hate them, and besides, this TV is black-and-white, not color."

This was too much for Stevie, who sprang to the defense of the little black-and-white television set the Quindlens kept in their spare room. "The *Three Stooges* are always in black and white," Stevie, a *Three Stooges* expert, informed Erica.

Erica made another one of her pickle faces and blew her nose.

"*Yeeee heh-heh,*" the girls heard one of the Three Stooges say, but only Stevie laughed. Even then she clamped her hand over her mouth so it wouldn't seem like she was having a good time when Erica and Molly were both so miserable.

Molly sat in the rocking chair in the corner of the room and wondered how long she and Stevie had to keep Erica company. While the images of the *Three Stooges* filled the screen, she kept one ear out for the van pulling into the driveway.

A half hour passed, and not one car came up Half Moon Lane. Finally, just as Moe was bopping Curly with a rolled newspaper, the phone rang, and Molly made a flying leap to get it in her room.

"Hello," she said into the mouthpiece the very moment that Mrs. Ames picked up the downstairs extension. "Mom, are you there?"

Mr. Quindlen was at the other end. "Sorry, sweetie, it's just me. Mom's getting X-rayed right now and said to tell you she'll be fine. Now why don't you let me talk to Judy?"

Molly tried to keep the hurt out of her voice.

"Okay, Dad." Why was it that when something bad happened, kids were the last to know? Molly put down the receiver and tiptoed downstairs to see if she could figure out from Mrs. Ames's end of the conversation what was happening to her mother.

"I see, Bill," Mrs. Ames was saying in a low voice. "Well, let's hope it turns out to be nothing. It's too bad when these things happen right around the holidays, but that's always the way. No, don't worry about a thing. I'll get the girls off to bed."

When Molly heard Mrs. Ames click down the kitchen phone, she went up the stairs as quietly as possible, stepping over the creaky steps. By the time Mrs. Ames came up, too, Molly was settled back in the rocking chair and pretending she was deeply involved in the *Three Stooges*.

"Well, I see you girls have found something to take your mind off things," Mrs. Ames said. "When this is over, would you turn it off and try to get to sleep? It's been a long night."

There were just a few minutes until the end of the program, and Molly spent them staring at the stolen Christmas socks, which Erica had the nerve to leave right on top of the duffel bag where everyone could see them. But it was late, and Molly was too tired to start up the Great Socks Battle again. It would have to wait until morning when her parents were home to referee. *If* they were home to referee.

"Come on, Stevie," Molly said when the movie credits came on.

"Could you please take your sneakers with you?" Erica said, looking down at Stevie's high-tops as if there were a dead mouse hiding in them.

Usually Stevie didn't mind people teasing her about her beat-up high-top sneakers, but tonight she minded. "Well, excuuuuse me!" she said, hugging the old sneakers to her chest. "I sure wouldn't want to make a mess of your neat room!"

With that, the girls were out the door, leaving Erica to fume in the guest room by herself.

"Erica always says something that gets me going and . . . hey, Molly, I'm sorry," Stevie apologized. "I know you're upset about your mom. I'm a jerk, but I'm a Friends 4-Ever jerk, so you have to put up with me."

"Thanks, Stevie," Molly said when they went back to her room to make up the floor mattress.

When Mrs. Ames came in a little later to check on the girls, she expected to hear the usual chattering and give them the usual sleepover warnings about this being absolutely the last time she was going to come in. Instead she found Stevie sound asleep, one leg hanging off the floor mattress. From the doorway, she could see Molly curled in the farthest corner of her bed next to the wall.

What Mrs. Ames couldn't see was Molly picking away at one of the little pink houses on her wallpaper. This was something she did when she was very upset, and over the years several rows of houses had lost their chimneys and roofs. Molly usually liked to think of happy families and good friends living in the wallpaper houses, but tonight she knew something terrible was happening inside one of them.

By the time she fell asleep, she had practically demolished an entire house.

6

LIGHTS, CURTAIN, DISASTER

The first thing Molly saw when she stepped from her bedroom the next morning was a foot — a red-and-green foot covered with spangled reindeer.

The foot belonged to Erica and so did the I-dare-you look she gave Molly when she emerged from the steamy bathroom. The reindeer socks, and the girl in them, skipped down the hall. Turning around to give Molly one more look, Erica said, "You'll find out tonight when my mother gets back that she bought me these, so there!"

"What *is* she talking about?" Stevie said when she stumbled out to the hall.

"Never mind," Molly answered. "I have to find out about my mother."

Molly ran downstairs, landing with a crash, and flew into the kitchen with the hope that her mother would be there sipping coffee and reading the newspaper. But the newspaper was still in its plastic wrapper, unread. Mr. Quindlen was staring into the refrigerator as if he hoped to find fully cooked breakfasts for everyone inside.

"What happened to Mom last night?" Molly wanted to know.

Her father yawned. "I'll tell you in a minute when I have my coffee and my eyeballs start working again."

"Mom? What happened to Mom?" Molly repeated.

"Well, it took three hours to get some antibiotics, and that'll clear up everything in a day or two if Mom takes it easy. The doctor told her to stay in bed today, so that's what she's doing."

"She's okay?" Molly asked, just to make sure.

"Not this minute, but what she has will clear up now that she has something to get rid of the bug," Mr. Quindlen said.

Molly didn't quite trust her dad in the morning. Like her, he was not a morning person. Sometimes he said things early in the day that came out crabby-sounding or just plain wrong. Not until she saw her mother up and about was Molly going to feel any better.

Just then, there was another crash, and Stevie, who *was* a morning person, popped into the kitchen. "Don't get up, Mr. Quindlen. I'll get myself some juice," she said. "I know where it is."

Mr. Quindlen managed a smile. "Finally, a guest who likes my orange juice and doesn't need room service," he whispered to Stevie in a low voice.

But not low enough.

"Don't worry, my parents are coming tonight," Erica announced as she came into the kitchen. "I talked to my mom on the phone before I went to bed last night, and she said she'll be back to see my dance performance at school tonight."

"The *Nutcracker*! It's tonight?" Molly cried.

"What do you think Suzi and I have been doing all these weeks?" Erica asked. "Of course, the one we put on at the school is really a sort of dress rehearsal. The *real* performance is in the city, in Providence, and people have to pay *ten* dollars a ticket."

Stevie picked up a spoon and began clicking it against her juice glass. "Woweee. In the big city. Ten dollars."

Erica gave Stevie the kind of look she would give a disgusting bug. "I think I'll skip breakfast," Erica said. "I'm supposed to meet Suzi early so we can discuss our costumes and things for tonight." With a loud sigh, she was gone.

"Phew, now I can eat without getting sick," Stevie said.

Molly had no thoughts of food, just of seeing her mother. "Dad, do you think Mom might be awake now? I have to ask her something."

"Mmm," Mr. Quindlen answered without really answering.

Molly took her untouched juice glass and raced upstairs without spilling a drop. She tiptoed into her parents' room and put the glass on the bedside table. "Mom? I brought you some juice."

Mrs. Quindlen opened her eyes, closed them, then opened them again. "Hmm. What time is it?" she asked in a sleepy voice.

"Almost eight," Molly answered. "Are you better?" she asked.

Mrs. Quindlen reached out for the juice and took several long gulps before answering. "Can't tell yet. It's too early, but I'm glad you came in. Are you feeling better, honey? You looked so upset last night, and I felt awful going to the hospital in such a rush."

Molly tried to act as if having her mother disappear to a hospital was the most normal thing in the world. "I'm okay," she lied. "Mom, is it true Erica is leaving tonight? She said her parents are coming back so they can be at the *Nutcracker* when it comes to our school. Do I *have* to go to it?"

With the back of her hand, Mrs. Quindlen felt her forehead. "Not so hot today," she mumbled. "The *Nutcracker*? Oh, honey, I think Erica would be very hurt if you didn't go. And just in case her parents can't make it back, she's going to need some family in the audience to cheer her on, don't you think?"

"But we're not her family," Molly protested. Then she saw the disappointed look on her mother's face.

"For now we are. Besides, I'm not in any shape to go, so I need you to take my place," Mrs. Quindlen said in a voice that made Molly

88

feel like shrinking and crawling away. "I'm counting on you."

Molly managed a half nod. "Sure, Mom," she answered.

That night nothing Molly tried would get the static out of her fine, flyaway hair. She had a good mind to run into the guest room and borrow some of the expensive goop Erica used to keep her hair looking perfect. But no, that would be stealing, just like Erica had stolen her socks. Well, maybe that was one good thing about *Nutcracker*. She would be able to tell Mrs. Soames about the missing socks.

Just as Molly was flattening her hair with the palm of her hand, Erica came into Molly's room, wrapped like a mummy in a towel. "Did my mother call while I was in the shower?" she asked, not noticing the wet footprints she was leaving on Molly's nice, white rug.

"Nope," Molly said.

"Maybe they're going to surprise me. Yes, that's it. Of course. And they'll have flowers for me," Erica mumbled to herself when she went back to the guest room to get into her costume.

"Yeah, a bouquet of Venus Flytraps," Molly

said after Erica closed the door. Then Molly went back to putting the finishing touches on her outfit. She dumped everything in her 'N Stuff box onto the bed and tried to decide what earrings went with her red turtleneck dress.

"Where are my jingle bell earrings anyway?" she said, trying to sort through stickers, ratty friendship bracelets, broken sand dollars, and ticket stubs from movies she couldn't remember anymore. Although there was a mound of odds and ends, Molly could not find the holiday earrings her neighbor, Mrs. Hansen, had given her for Christmas. And when she poked through the stray pop beads and seed pods she could see something even more important was missing: a lucky rock Stevie had given her a couple years before. Someone had been in the 'N Stuff box, and Molly had a pretty good idea who it was.

She marched across the hall and banged on Erica's door.

"Mom? Are you back?" Erica cried. "Come in! I'm doing my warm-up exercises."

When Molly opened the door, Erica was the Sugar Plum Fairy herself, although one with a very stylish wedge haircut. She was bent all the way forward over one leg she had stretched out on the edge of the bed. Slowly, she rose then turned, with a big smile for her mother.

Molly couldn't help it. The sight of the rose-colored tutu sprinkled with silvery stars made her sick with jealousy. She stood there, with her empty 'N Stuff box in hand, and just stared.

"Oh, it's you," Erica said changing from the Sugar Plum Fairy into a disappointed, then angry girl right before Molly's eyes. "I thought you were my mother."

"Well, I'm not," Molly said, sure that her brown eyes must look bright green to Erica as she kept staring at the beautiful costume. "I'm missing some earrings and some other stuff from this box, and I wonder if you took — I mean packed them — by mistake."

Erica stroked her diamond-studded earlobes with her fingertips. "Why would I want your earrings when I have diamond ones? As for touching anything in that thing," she said, glancing at the beat-up 'N Stuff box, "I'd be afraid to catch a disease. And I'm getting a little tired of you always accusing me of taking things. Anyway, I'm going home, so you'll have to blame somebody else after tonight."

Molly shook the empty box at her. "Well, you took our toothpaste the first night you were here, and I *saw* you in this box the other day. And,"

Molly stopped to take a deep breath, "you had on socks just like mine, which have been missing ever since you got here."

Erica fluffed up her tutu like an angry bird ruffling its feathers. "I am not going to talk to someone so *juvenile*. Ask my mother about the socks. She got them for me on a business trip. As for the other stuff, why would I want a lot of old, used junk anyway?"

"It's not junk!" Molly protested before a car horn interrupted her.

Erica threw on her ski jacket, which, amazingly, matched the tutu. Grabbing her dance bag, she glided past Molly like a ballerina making a farewell exit.

"Molly? Molly?" Mrs. Quindlen called from the bedroom. "Did Erica just leave? A pink blur just waved good night and then disappeared."

Molly went into her parents' room where her mother and father were watching the news and Scotty was playing racetrack at the foot of the bed. "Suzi Taylor's father just came to get her."

"Aw, I was hoping to see how she looked since I have to miss the performance," Mrs. Quindlen said. "You look pretty in that turtleneck dress. Want a spritz of perfume? Bill, can you get my perfume from the dresser?"

Molly was so glad to see her mother looking better, she tried to put Erica and the tutu out of her thoughts. She did a little pirouette as her Mom squirted her with a bit of perfume.

"Sounds like your limo is here," Mr. Quindlen joked when he heard the Ryders' horn toot. "Now, off you go and have a good time."

"I'll try," Molly said, but she was going to have to try awfully hard.

Stevie started talking the second Molly slid into the backseat of the Ryders' car. "If you see Mike, would you guys do me a favor and don't mention it?"

"Mike?" Laura shrieked from the front seat. "At a ballet?"

Stevie leaned forward to shush Laura. "Don't even say those words in the same breath or else I'll be carsick. He said he and some guys from the hockey team might show up to watch after practice. I told him if he does he could be the Nutcracker Prince since I think he's nuts for following the Know-It-Alls around."

Everyone in the car laughed at Stevie's joke. They all knew how much she hated sharing her brothers with any girl.

"Last stop!" Mr. Ryder called when he pulled up in front of the Crispin Landing Elementary

School auditorium. "Laura, call me when it's over, and I'll come pick you up."

When the girls got out of the car, Molly couldn't believe how many people were streaming into the auditorium. "I guess some people didn't want to pay ten dollars to see this in Providence when they can watch it for free here," she said.

Laura linked her arm through Molly's so they could comfort each other. "Well, don't anybody clap too hard," Laura told everyone. "I don't think I'll be able to stand it, knowing Molly and I could have been up there if our parents didn't treat us like babies."

"Don't worry, guys, I'm not going to clap at all," Stevie said loyally. "Oh, no! There's Mike."

The girls had to pass Mike and some of his middle school buddies on the way in, so when Stevie turned her head away from them, the other girls did the same.

"Honestly, I might do a Donald Duck quack in the middle of the ballet," Stevie threatened. "Or tie their toe shoes in knots so they can't get them on."

"Or put Super Glue on the stage, so they get stuck," Meg cackled. Both girls knew how hard it must be for Molly and Laura to be on the audience side of the stage when they could have been on the other side.

"Never mind glue," Stevie interrupted. "How about liquid soap so Erica could try out her ice-dancing instead of her stupid ballet?"

"Ballet isn't stupid," Molly protested. Stevie's and Meg's ideas for pranks were funny, but she and Laura *loved* ballet.

"It's beautiful," Laura breathed in agreement.

Molly tried hard not to notice the dancers' feet scampering behind the curtain, which didn't quite reach the stage floor. Oh, how she longed to be on that side of the curtain in those few minutes before it went up and everything had to be perfect! How was she going to sit through this and watch Erica up there instead?

The house lights flickered off and on, off and on, off and on.

"I bet that's Josh Brown," Stevie whispered. "My brother Dave knows him. He does all the audiovisual stuff at the high school and always flicks the lights a million times to get everybody seated and quiet."

The flickering lights actually did settle down the audience, and soon the lights went up on the cozy holiday scene that opened the *Nutcracker*. Within minutes, Molly completely forgot where she was and got caught up in the thrilling music.

She was actually able to enjoy the first half of the ballet since Erica wasn't due to come on until after the intermission. She had to admit, as the first half ended with the snowflake dancers, that a professional company like the New England Ballet made the dances even more beautiful. Only a tap on the shoulder pulled her out of the trance she was in.

"Look up!" Stevie signaled to Molly to crane her head to the catwalk over the stage where Josh was now dropping flakes of paper or soap flakes onto the stage to make it look like a snowfall.

The audience ooooed and aaahed in appreciation, but only for a few seconds.

"Omigosh, look!" Molly cried along with a lot of people when the audience saw one of the snowflake dancers slip and fall.

It was an especially terrible moment for Laura and Molly, who could imagine all too well how horribly embarrassed the ballerina must feel. But whoever she was, the dancer knew what to do. She got herself up gracefully and joined the line of snowflake dancers as best she could.

A sigh of relief went through the audience,

but it didn't last. A second ballerina skidded, but caught herself just in time. By the time the house lights went up for intermission, everyone was glad to get out of their seats for a while.

"Phew, I thought they were playing hockey in there for a while," Stevie joked when the girls went out to the lobby. "I hope that wasn't part of the show."

"Steeeevie!" Molly protested. "Josh must have thrown down too many snowflakes from the catwalk, and it made the stage slippery. How would you like that to happen to you?"

Stevie did a pretend ballet twirl and almost toppled over. "Sheesh, I thought you'd be glad to see the Know-It-Alls' dance group goof up."

Molly couldn't help laughing, and all the tension she'd felt while watching the ill-fated snowflake dance dissolved into a fit of laughs. She and Laura, then Stevie and Meg, passed the intermission time pretending to be graceful ballerinas who kept slipping on invisible things.

Before the auditorium lights flicked off and on for everyone to go back inside, Molly searched the crowd for the Soameses. Maybe she could get the sock business straightened out while Erica was backstage instead of waiting for later when Erica was going to be queen of the *Nut cracker*. Molly saw Shana and some other kids she knew, but the Soameses were nowhere to be seen. By the time Molly went back to her seat she had decided they were probably backstage fussing over Erica, whose big number was coming up in the second half of the show.

"Where's Stevie?" Meg whispered as the lights in the auditorium dimmed and Stevie's seat was still empty.

Laura and Molly swiveled around to see if their friend was coming in late, but everyone was seated and waiting expectantly for the curtain to go up. When it did, they all gasped at the beauty of the candy shop set decorated in gumdrop, chocolate, lollipop, and ice-cream colors.

It was breathtaking, and Molly longed to be waiting in the wings, ready to go on as anything, even a dancing chocolate. She had never seen such beautiful sets during any performance at her school. Just as Erica had kept saying, everything looked so *professional*.

Except for one thing.

When Molly craned her neck to see how tall the sets were she spotted Josh Brown up on the catwalk again. And right next to him was, of all people, Stevie! Molly tapped Meg, then Laura, and pointed to the stage ceiling.

All three girls were so shocked, they could hardly breathe. They knew Stevie, the prankster, all too well. She was likely to start quacking or throwing down snowflakes any minute! To their relief, the music began, then played on with nothing unusual happening. No snowflakes fell during the candy shop scene; no Donald Duck voices cried out. The worst things that happened, which no one but the Friends 4-Ever could see, were Stevie's occasional devilish smiles and little waves.

The music built up to one of Molly's favorite pieces of music, the "Waltz of the Flowers." She could almost imagine what Erica was feeling as she waited for her own music to come on next. The "Dance of the Sugar Plum Fairy" music began, and Erica appeared, moving to the center of the stage in a graceful *pas de bourrée*. Now Molly was sure that not just her eyes but her whole body must be green with envy. She forgot all about Stevie and Josh up on the catwalk and focused on her soon-to-be-ex-houseguest.

When Erica raised her leg for her final turn on one leg, Molly wondered, like anyone who had studied ballet, how long she could turn.

Not long.

"Oh!" the audience gasped just a fraction of a second after Erica's supporting leg slid out from under her and she landed with a terrible thud on the stage. This time, there were no rows of other dancers to disappear into. Erica lay on the stage like a broken puppet.

The taped music whined to a stop, and the ballet mistress came out to rescue her fallen fairy. Molly could see Erica holding her leg and bowing her head way down, as if she wanted to shrink into a small ball that could just be rolled offstage.

The ballet mistress waved and waved up at Josh on the catwalk, signaling him to lower the curtain, please lower the curtain. Josh and Stevie looked at each other in complete confusion, not understanding what the ballet mistress's hand motions meant. Finally the curtain came down on the terrible scene.

"I don't believe it," Laura choked. "It's so horrible. I just about died."

"Me, too," Meg said. "And I don't even like her."

Molly was frozen in a strange kind of embarrassment, as if the whole thing had happened to her. Even a nightmare wouldn't be as awful as having the whole town see you have an accident onstage.

"I'm going backstage," she said over the announcement that the performance would resume in five minutes.

With Molly heading up the stage steps and behind the curtain, Meg and Laura followed. Backstage, dancing gumdrops, snowflake dancers, and dancers in mouse costumes clustered around a sobbing Erica.

"Somebody threw something down from the catwalk. That's why I tripped," she cried, though no one but Molly and her friends were listening.

The ballet mistress seemed to forget all about Erica as she ordered the rest of her dancers to take their places again. "Suzi! Suzi Taylor! Help Erica to the girls' room. She can lend you her costume, and you can finish out her part since you're the same size and you know the part. Dancers! Dancers! Resume positions for Variation 1!"

Molly threaded through the dancers who immediately forgot all about Erica and started doing their stretches and warm-ups until the music went on.

When Molly pushed open the door to the girls'

room, she could hear Erica crying, her sobs bouncing off the porcelain sinks and the tile walls and floors. The sound went up another decibel when Erica noticed that Molly had come into the room.

Molly watched Erica take off her pink ballet slippers and toss them on the floor. "Erica, I'm sorry."

Erica's eyes flashed with pain, but not the pain of a hurt leg. "How dare you follow me in here and say you're sorry! It was your friend, Stevie, who made me fall, and you and your friends probably put her up to it."

Molly turned to look at Laura and Meg who were right behind. Like Molly, they looked shocked, but unlike Molly they didn't believe for a second that Stevie had had anything to do with Erica's spill. But Molly couldn't get Stevie's threats out of her head. Hadn't she joked about putting nuts on the stage, about dumping a pail of snowflakes, or pouring glue on the stage? Hadn't Erica fallen right after Stevie went up on the catwalk where she had no business being? Better than anyone, Stevie knew how miserable Molly had been about Erica. Maybe she thought this was the way to make Molly feel better.

Molly felt ripped in two. In front of her was

a girl she had never liked, but who had gone from being the star of the ballet to a collapsed, defeated girl. Her parents had not shown up, and now her closest friend was waiting for her to hand over her costume and take over her big part. Molly, whose feelings never came in small doses but in raging floods, knew just how awful Erica must feel.

But Stevie? Stevie was a kidder, but she wasn't cruel.

As if on cue, the next voice that echoed in the cold, green-tiled bathroom was Stevie's. "Hey, you guys. I've been looking all over for you." She stopped when she saw Erica pulling on her street clothes. "Oh. Sorry about your spill."

The girls' bathroom was quiet except for the *drip, drip, drip* of a faucet.

"Don't speak to me," Erica shrieked. "Just go away! All of you! This is the worst night of my whole life."

7

SICK OF BEING SORRY

Out of all the girls, Stevie Ames was the one
who had the fattest, tallest supply of Friends 4-
Ever stationery. She liked to *do* things, not write
about them, and everyone thought she would
be an old lady and still have a huge box of
sneaker stationery left. But in the days after the
Nutcracker, she made a big dent in her supply.
Every time Molly, Meg, and Laura checked their
mail spots over the weekend, there was a note
from Stevie explaining over and over that she
hadn't caused Erica Soames's onstage disaster.

Molly was just taking the backyard shortcut
from her house to Meg's late Sunday afternoon

when she saw yet another piece of Stevie's sneaker stationery tucked into her own mail spot, the hook where the Quindlens hung their hammock every summer.

"Poor Stevie," she said, reading the note through before she noticed the words: *Please give this to Erica as soon as possible.*

Dear Erica,

I asked Molly a zillion times to give you this message: I'M SORRY ABOUT WHAT HAPPENED AT YOUR DANCE. But since you won't talk to me on the phone or in person, I'm writing this note.

I did not, repeat, I did not drop anything onstage to make you fall down, and neither did Josh. Even the ballet leader said she thought the fake snowflakes made the dancers slip. Too bad you had such a horrible fall. I know this is worse than when you made your duck voice at the rehearsal. That's why you have to believe me. If you don't, then my friends won't believe me, either.

Last fall at a big soccer game I twisted my ankle in front of practically the whole world. So I know how it feels. Horrible. I would never make something that awful happen to anybody, not even my worst enemy! Please believe me.

I'm Sorry x 1,000,000,000

STEVIE AMES

"Read this," Molly said when she got to the Milanos' house, and Meg was there waiting for her at the back door. "It's just the saddest thing."

Meg took the note and then led Molly down to the basement rec room. The Friends 4-Ever were going to practice Molly's play one last time before the school assembly the next morning, if Stevie showed up, that is. Both girls plopped down on the old plaid couch, not the least bit interested in trying on their old-fashioned costumes or rehearsing their lines. Instead, Meg read over Stevie's note to Erica. When she finished, she looked at Molly. "So what do you think Erica will do with this?"

"Tear it into a million pieces," Molly answered

without any doubt in her voice. "She hung up on Stevie twice when she called to explain. I showed her the notes Stevie sent me, but she handed them right back. It's horrible, and it's ruining everything. No matter what I say, Erica thinks we all had something to do with what happened. I don't even get a chance to explain since she's been at Suzi's half the time or shut up in the guest room ever since the *Nutcracker*."

Meg stared at her clipboard list of things the girls had to do, but there was nothing on there about how to straighten out the Erica Soames Stew they were all in now. "Can't your parents do something?"

Molly sighed. "They keep reminding me how miserable Erica must be since her parents still aren't back. Besides, my mom's still sick, so I can't bug her too much."

"I can't believe the Soameses didn't make it back for the ballet, especially after telling Erica they would be there. They never miss anything she's in. They're always in the front row with their video camera and blocking everybody's view. Why aren't they back yet?"

"I have no idea," Molly groaned. "My parents still won't tell me what they're doing in Boston for so long. Probably making tons of money."

Molly looked toward the stairs where the girls heard footsteps.

"Hi, Laura," Meg said. "Hi, Shana. Where's Stevie? I thought she was coming with you."

Shana sighed. "I stopped by her house, and she told me she wasn't coming."

Laura looked a little nervous about upsetting Molly. "She just called and said she wanted to wait at home in case Erica called her. I told her I didn't think there was much chance of that, but she said she'd wait anyway. She told me she sent Erica a note, but so far she hasn't heard from her. By the way, now Stevie thinks we don't believe her, either!"

"Of course we believe her," Meg said, sorting through the costume bag to get herself in the mood for this meeting. "Right, Molly?"

Molly didn't answer.

"Right, Molly?" Meg repeated.

Molly swallowed hard and tried to say something that was hard to get out. "Did you ever think maybe she *did* do something to make Erica fall?"

Shana stared down at her neon sneakers. She wasn't about to get mixed up in this argument.

Laura's eyes widened with shock. "How *can*

you even think that, Molly?" Laura asked. "How can you?"

Molly couldn't quite look at her friends. "I don't mean she did it on purpose. But maybe she went up to the catwalk just to fool around so that Laura and I would feel better about not being in the ballet. You know how Stevie is. Anyway, maybe she was going to *pretend* to drop something, not really do it, but she dropped something on the stage by mistake."

"Thanks a whole lot, Molly!" the girls heard next from the basement stairs right before the cellar door slammed shut. Meg raced up and just managed to catch Stevie by the back of her hockey jacket before she got out the back door.

"I'm not letting go of your jacket until you come down and see us," Meg said as Stevie struggled to get out of her jacket and escape.

But Meg was too quick and somehow pulled a wriggling Stevie downstairs where the other girls were waiting.

Molly and Stevie stared at each other like two strange animals and not at all like the close friends they really were.

"I knew I shouldn't have come over," Stevie said. "I knew, I just knew, you thought I did something to Erica on purpose." Stevie was trying hard to look mad and not sad, but the misery was all over her face. "You don't believe me, do you, Molly?"

Molly couldn't lie. "I believe you didn't *mean* to do anything to Erica on purpose, but maybe by accident something happened that you couldn't help. You *were* up on the catwalk. I'm sorry, but that's what I can't figure out."

Stevie wiped her eyes with the raggedy cotton cuffs of her jacket. "I just thought it would be funny to be up there while Erica was prancing around. That's all, I swear. Why are you taking *her* side, anyway?"

The other four girls faced Molly.

"I'm not taking her side, not really," Molly answered. "It's just that you don't have to see her every day like I do or be nice to her the way my parents want me to. They keep saying they'll tell me why after her parents come and get her, but I'm stuck with her now, and she thinks we all ruined her dance. Everything's a mess."

Meg Milano, who hated any kind of mess, tried to pull her friends together. "Look, guys, it doesn't matter what made Erica have her accident. We have to put on our skit tomorrow, and we can't do that if we're going to stand around fighting about Erica. She's not worth it."

"Amen!" Laura said, but no one else joined in.

"Oh, all right," Molly agreed, but her heart wasn't in it. In fact, she didn't know where her heart was. After a long, silent minute she picked up her script. In a quiet, non-Molly voice, she gave the girls their directions. "Okay, Meg, you stand there. Laura and Shana over there. Stevie, stand on the stairs with the flashlight."

The girls did as they were told and tried to pretend that they were a happy prairie family in the 1800s. But the five grumpy friends acted out their parts like robots. They knew where to stand, they knew what to say, but there was not a bit of warm feeling in the chilly basement that afternoon.

All the way home, Molly talked to herself, but the words she recited were not from her play. "If I give her Stevie's note, she'll just throw it away and get mad at me besides." She kicked at the old root of the tree in her backyard. "And if I don't, she'll just stay mad like she is already."

"You all set for tomorrow morning?" Mr. Quindlen said when Molly came into the house.

Molly didn't hear him.

"Hey, I think I can sneak out after my first class and get to your skit tomorrow after all," Mr. Quindlen said to get Molly's attention. "I don't think Mom's going to make it. She's still on the mend, and Dr. McDade says don't push things too soon. But I'll be there, front row, center."

"Good," Molly finally answered, not really paying attention to her father's news. "Is Erica back from Suzi's yet?"

"She just got back a little while ago," Mr. Quindlen whispered. "She's been on the phone with her mother for a while, poor kid."

Molly kicked off one boot so hard, it flew across the kitchen floor. What was this "poor kid" stuff all the time, anyway? Erica was allowed to do this and do that just because her parents were away.

Molly rescued her stray boot and threw it down with its mate. "Why is she a poor kid now?"

"Hey, Molly Melinda," Mr. Quindlen said. "Wouldn't you be homesick if we stuck you someplace you didn't want to be *and* we missed a big event of yours? Think about how upset you were just this morning when you found out Mom couldn't go see your skit tomorrow."

This was true, but Molly wasn't in any mood to go over *that* again. Anyway, she and Erica had *nothing* in common, and she didn't want anybody to think they did.

"I'm going upstairs," she told her dad. "I have something for Erica."

The door to the guest room was open a few inches, and Erica was still talking on the phone. As usual, she was so loud, Molly could hear every word of a not-too-happy conversation.

"The whole town saw me fall, everybody," Erica cried.

Molly waited, not even trying to listen to the umpteenth conversation about the *Nutcracker* fiasco. Honestly, there was going to be a thousand-dollar phone bill by the time everyone finished talking about it!

"I didn't have anybody to talk to afterward," Erica went on, "and I had to come *here*. Molly hates me, I can just tell, so she got her friends to ruin my *whole* dance."

Erica stopped talking so she could blow her nose. "I just don't understand why you and Daddy have to stay so long in Boston! It's like your business is more important than I am!" she finally said. "Anyway, I want to go to stay at

113

Suzi's, starting tonight. I don't care if I have to sleep on the floor! So call the Quindlens and tell them!"

Molly waited a long minute after Erica hung up before she knocked on the door.

And Erica waited an even longer time before she answered. "Who is it?" she shouted.

"Me," Molly answered. "Can I come in?"

"No."

Molly knocked again. "I have something to give you," she said through the crack in the door.

"If it's one of those dumb notes from you and your friends, forget it. It's too late. You've ruined everything already!"

Molly pushed the door open a few inches more and did her best to feel sorry for Erica. "Please read this. It's from Stevie."

Molly, it turned out, had been wrong when she'd told Meg that Erica would tear the note into a million pieces. She didn't tear it up at all. She just wadded it into a tight ball and tossed it into the wastebasket where it joined a mountain of used tissues.

"Nothing your little club says can make up for what happened," Erica said. "Now, do you mind? I have to pack. I'm not staying in your house another night. I'm going someplace where people will be nice to me!"

This was too much for Molly. Hadn't the Quindlens offered their house to Erica and let her do whatever she wanted, letting her come home any old time and making her special meals so she wouldn't have allergy attacks? Hadn't poor Riggs been banished to the downstairs so he wouldn't get hair on Erica's things? Wasn't Molly's very own mother sick as a dog ever since Erica had arrived? Molly clenched her nails into the palms of ther hands as her feeling-sorry-for-Erica mood evaporated.

Molly made a move toward one of Erica's duffel bags. "Maybe I can help you pack!"

Erica pushed the duffel bag away with her foot. "Don't you dare touch any of my things!"

"You should talk since you're wearing *my* socks!" Molly snapped back. "Then maybe *my* mother will get better once she doesn't have to worry about you and whether you have enough towels!"

Erica began throwing jewelry, underwear, sweatshirts, and shoes into her luggage. "It's not my fault your mother got a cold right after I got here."

Molly's heart was pounding now. Somehow,

whatever was wrong with her mother had arrived the day Erica did. "It's not just a cold, I'll have you know. My mom is sick, real sick. She's been going to the doctor's, and I've heard her saying she might have to have tests to find out if she's got — " Molly stopped before she named any of the awful diseases she had read about in the medical book. What if saying their names made her mother actually have one of them? Before she could gather her thoughts, she saw Erica slowly sink to the bed, dropping a nightshirt on the floor.

"It's not your mother who's sick, you know that?" she said in a quiet voice. "It's mine."

Erica's words hung in the air like smoke after an explosion. Molly felt a tiny flicker of relief, and then a longer, slower feeling she didn't like. Shame.

"What do you mean?" Molly managed to ask.

Erica pushed back her bangs with her hand as if to push away a terrible headache or a fever. "When you overheard your mother talking, she was talking to my mother, that's what I mean. Now it all makes sense. I couldn't figure out why my parents had to go to Boston. They wouldn't do that right before I was going to be in the *Nutcracker*, I just know they wouldn't. The day they left, I took a phone message from a hospital in Boston, and the person said to call back, that an appointment had opened up. My mother tried not to let on, and I didn't really think about it. All I cared about was having to come over here, so I didn't pay any attention to why my parents had to leave so fast."

Erica sat on the bed, twisting one of the many rings she always wore. Molly couldn't believe how even the cool Providence haircut, the great leggings outfit, and the diamond earrings didn't keep Erica from looking like a lost, miserable girl.

Molly forced herself to ignore all her anger at Erica, and sat down on the bed next to her. "I'm sorry. I'm really sorry if your mother is sick with something bad. Boy, do I ever know what that feels like after what I'd been thinking all this time."

Erica moved to the end of the bed as if Molly was yet another thing she was allergic to. "Well, you must be relieved and glad it's my mother, not yours, who had to go to the hospital for real and not just because she had a cold!"

Molly knew she deserved that, and a tiny part of what Erica said was true. She *was* relieved her own mother was okay. Still, at that moment, she felt truly sorry for Erica.

"I'm not glad it's your mother," Molly said truthfully. "I wish it wasn't anybody. I mean it."

"Thanks, but no thanks," Erica answered. "It doesn't change anything, not my mother, not the way you ruined my ballet, not the way you accused me of wrecking your skit and taking things out of your room. That only makes everything ten times worse."

Erica grabbed the giant teddy bear she had brought to the Quindlens and sobbed into it like it was the only friend she had in the world.

"Girls, girls, what is it?" Molly heard someone say. "I hope you two aren't arguing on Erica's last night here."

When Erica and Molly turned around, Mrs. Quindlen was standing in the room. To Molly, she looked like a new mother, or rather like a new version of her old mother. Mrs. Quindlen had put on her red-and-white snowflake sweater, and her cheeks looked rosy instead of gray for a change.

Erica squinted at Mrs. Quindlen suspiciously. "What do you mean, it's my last night here? Did my mom say it was okay to sleep over at Suzi's dad's apartment?"

Mrs. Quindlen smiled. "No, your parents are coming home late tomorrow morning. It's defi-

118

nite this time. Your mother said she'll pick you up at school at lunchtime and take you out to celebrate."

Erica's red eyes looked a little brighter. "Celebrate what?"

"Well, she'll give you all the details, but now that everything has worked out okay, I guess I can tell you. Your parents were very worried about your mother's health and went up to Boston so she could have some medical tests. But when I just called, she said there's absolutely nothing wrong with her. She says she's just fine and to tell you that in case you wondered what was going on. Oh, and one other thing, she wanted to know if there's anything you would like her to bring back from Boston."

Erica flung back her head, and her bangs fell perfectly across her forehead. "Anything?" She pulled on one of her earrings. "Hmm. I wonder if there's a bracelet to match these."

A SURPRISE SWITCH

Molly lay in bed before her alarm went off and giggled at the thought that she was already dressed for her *Little House on the Prairie* skit. She snuggled under her quilt and pulled her flannel nightgown around her. At that moment she wasn't such a different girl than Laura Ingalls who had slept under a quilt and worn a flannel nightgown so long ago.

There was one difference, though. In the 1800s, Laura Ingalls didn't have a telephone ringing in her room as Molly Quindlen did this morning. The ringing jolted her out of her cozy thoughts, and she reached over to pick up the phone before the whole house woke up.

"Hello," she said in a gravelly voice. "Mrs. Milano? Is it a snow day or something?" she asked. Why on earth was Meg's mother calling the Quindlens at six o'clock in the morning?

But, no, it wasn't a snow day. That would have been fun. This was something that wasn't fun at all.

"But Meg was fine yesterday when we practiced at your house," Molly said, her voice rising with worry. "She didn't seem sick at all." How could Meg be sick, today of all days? In just a few hours she was supposed to play the part of Mary Ingalls. "Can she come to the phone?" Molly asked desperately.

No, Meg Milano could not come to the phone. She was asleep and much too sick with the flu to talk to anyone.

Molly heard a knock at the door, and her mother came in. "Who were you talking to, honey? I thought it was a wrong number."

"I wish it were a wrong number," Molly said miserably. "Meg can't be in my skit. She's got a high fever, and her mother won't let her go to school." Molly was sure if it weren't for such a thing as parents Meg would have been in the play no matter what.

Mrs. Quindlen sat down on the bed next to Molly who was still gripping the phone in case Mrs. Milano called back to say Meg had recovered in the last five minutes. "Oh, Molly, that's awful." Mrs. Quindlen put her arm around Molly's shoulders. "I'm so sorry. Well, let's think. Maybe Stevie could take Meg's part. She's been rehearsing with you."

"Stevie has to do the spotlight," Molly said. "Besides she doesn't really know all the words, just the cues to move the spotlight." Couldn't Mrs. Milano see the whole thing was ruined, positively ruined? "There isn't going to be any skit. We can't do it without Meg!"

Molly bolted from her bed and ran to the bathroom so she could have a good cry with the water running full blast. But, of course, early as it was, Erica was already in there with her lotions, potions, and piles of towels.

"Sorry," Molly said when she burst in on Erica brushing her teeth. "I didn't know you were in here already."

"What's the matter? Your eyes are all puffy. I have some cucumber lotion somewhere in here that's good for getting rid of puffy eyes," Erica said, trying for once to be helpful. "Were you nervous about your skit? I usually can't sleep either the night before I have to go onstage."

Molly looked up at Erica, surprised that she admitted getting the jitters before a performance. Was it possible that someone who used three kinds of skin lotion was a real person inside?

"I'm not going onstage," Molly told her. "So it doesn't matter if I have puffy eyes."

"Did they cancel the Holiday Concert?" Erica asked. "Boy, Mrs. Higgle will have a fit."

Molly sat down on the edge of the tub and picked at some fuzz on the bathroom rug. "Meg can't be in the play. She's got the flu, and her mother won't let her go to school, so we can't do my play. There's no one else who can do her part."

Erica stopped brushing her hair. "I'm really sorry. Honestly. After what happened to me with the *Nutcracker*, do I ever know what it's like to have something ruined that you've been practicing."

Yeah, sure, Molly thought, remembering just who it was who had ruined her play rehearsal.

"You still think I interrupted your play when you were rehearsing it, don't you?"

Molly nodded. "Sort of. It looked like you and

Suzi, and it was around the time you were coming back from your rehearsals in Providence, so you didn't have to be in class."

Erica turned away from Molly, hurt and a little angry, too. "All I can say is we didn't do it. I don't know how to make you believe me." Erica leaned into the mirror and began her daily eyebrow smoothing. "I didn't ruin your play, no matter what you think, but I do know how to save it."

Molly stopped picking at the rug fuzz and looked up at Erica. "What do you mean?"

"*I* could play Meg's part," Erica announced. "I not only have blonde hair, but I have a photographic memory."

Molly tried not to groan. As Erica was always saying whenever there was a test at school, she never had to study since she could memorize information by reading it once. In fact, she had won a trip to Washington, D.C., by coming in first in the Geography Bee a few months back thanks to her famous "photographic memory."

When Molly didn't answer right away, Erica said in a soft voice, "Oh, Laura. This has been the best Christmas ever. We have a cup and a cake *and* a penny."

Those were some of the lines from the book

that Molly had put in her skit. But a Know-It-All playing the part of sweet, quiet Mary Ingalls? Molly had a hard time with that thought. "The character's supposed to have long, blonde hair, and yours is short."

Erica sighed, then went right back to her eyebrow brushing. "Well, look, I'm not going to beg. I just thought I'd offer since I've been staying in your house and all, but just forget it."

Molly saw the last chance for performing her skit about to disappear. "Well, I suppose you could wear a nightcap or something to cover your hair."

"Good," Erica answered. "While you're getting ready for school, I'll read over the script. I can look at something once and know it by heart ten minutes later, you know."

"I know, I know," Molly said. She could already picture Erica bragging all over school how, thanks to her incredible photographic memory, she saved Molly's little skit at the last minute. What a sickening thought. But it wasn't quite as sickening as no skit at all. "Oh, well," Molly said. "The show must go on."

"Honestly," Laura whispered to Erica as both of them, along with Molly and Shana, watched

125

the sword dancers stumble through their folk dance. "I wish someone would let the curtain down. It's too horrible to watch."

Laura and Erica had hardly ever spoken to each other before today, but as excellent dancers themselves, they could hardly stand to see the four dancers constantly tripping over their swords when they were supposed to be doing dance steps in between them. Before the dance was halfway through, two of the four cardboard swords were twisted out of shape from constantly being stepped on.

"At least it was fake snowflakes that caused my fall," Erica said, not actually saying whether she still thought the Friends 4-Ever had had something to do with it.

At last, to everyone's relief, the sword dance music came to an end, and the four dancers ran off the stage. While everyone was clapping, Shana and Laura dashed out from the wings, put up a cardboard fireplace, and hung two stockings from it. Molly and Erica scooted out with a small table and placed an old-fashioned pitcher in the middle of it.

Everything was ready. Molly looked up at Stevie on the catwalk and gave her the signal to start the tape of "I Will Bow and Be Simple," a country song that sounded to Molly like something Pa Ingalls might play on his fiddle at Christmastime.

"Ready, everybody?" Molly whispered.

Laura, who was going to play Mrs. Ingalls, checked that her bun was neat and her apron was on straight. Erica made sure her wedge haircut was tucked into the white bonnet Molly had given her so she would look more like a girl from the 1800s. Molly signaled frantically to Shana that she still had on one parrot earring.

When Molly stepped onto the stage, Stevie's spotlight followed her slowly and accurately as she made her way to the fake fireplace and pulled down one of the knit stockings. A minute later Erica came out and did the same.

With the lovely fiddle music playing softly in the background, Erica and Molly said their lines without missing a syllable. The play went on just as smoothly as if Meg had been there, and Molly was almost completely caught up in the feeling of really *being* Laura Ingalls.

Almost. When Erica got to the lines just ahead of the ones about the stockings and the tin cups, Molly came back to the twentieth century. What if some of the other Know-It-Alls did the Donald Duck voice this time?

Her voice a little trembly, Molly said: "Look, Mary, we have our very own tin cups!"

She heard a couple of titters in the audience right then, but instead of the play stopping like last time, Erica smoothly said her next lines and saved the day. "Yes, Laura, we do. And a whole penny of our very own, and a cake, and even a stick of candy."

Hearing those words, Molly flew back in time again to talk with her prairie sister. By the time Shana and Laura came out as Ma and Pa Ingalls, the audience was totally silent and listening to every beautiful line of Molly's skit. Molly poured water from a pitcher on the table into her character's tin cup. This was Stevie's cue to lower the lights and stop the tape. To the last haunting notes of "I Will Bow and Be Simple," the curtain came down, and the audience broke into loud applause.

"They liked it," Molly breathed as she waited for the curtain to go up again. When it did, all four girls made graceful bows in front of their cheering classmates. Molly didn't even mind that Greg Egan, a Crispin Landing boy who often made fun of the Friends 4-Ever, was whistling and stomping like he was at a Red Sox game.

"Let's stay in our costumes a little while," Erica told Laura, Shana, and Molly.

They needed no convincing. Practically the whole point of being in a show was keeping the makeup and costumes on for as long as possible before joining the real world again.

Molly saw her father making his way through the crowds of kids who had sneaked away from their assigned seats to congratulate the performers. Above all the racket, Mrs. Higgle tried but failed to get everyone back to their seats so that everyone could watch the principal give her a bouquet of flowers. But it was too late. No one was watching or listening when Mrs. Higgle gave her little speech about the show.

"The play was super, Molly, just super," Mr. Quindlen said. He handed Molly some red and white carnations. "Mom told me to give you these. I only wish I'd thought to rent a video camera so she could see what a great job you did."

At that, Mr. and Mrs. Soames stepped up to the girls. Mr. Soames waved an expensive-looking camera at everyone. "Don't worry. We got everything on tape, Bill. Of course, we had to persuade a few people to give up their front row seats, but what good's one of these cameras if you can't be right in the front?"

Mrs. Soames was actually crying, whether from Molly's skit or from seeing Erica for the first time in a week, nobody knew. "Oh, darling! You were so wonderful, so sweet and gentle, just like Mary Ingalls! Don't you think so, girls?"

When Stevie started rolling her eyes and looked as if she were about to say something outrageous, Molly stepped on her foot.

"Yes, Erica was great," Molly answered. "She saved my play."

Mrs. Soames couldn't seem to stop her head from bobbing up and down in happiness. "Yes, my Erica has a photographic memory. You can give her something, and in a few minutes, she's committed it to memory."

Molly turned away as Mrs. Soames began a recitation about the Geography Bee, the Gifted and Special Program tests, and all the big things Erica had memorized with her stupendous memory. Molly giggled a little with Stevie, Laura, and Shana. It was hard to stand there and listen to the entire list of Erica Soames's accomplishments. But they did. After all, she had come to the rescue.

Mrs. Soames managed to tear herself away from her brilliant daughter long enough to hand a small, flat package to Molly.

"This is just a little present for letting Erica stay at your house. I bought Erica the same ones a few weeks back. You can only find them in Providence or Boston, you know."

"Or Kansas," Molly whispered in embarrassment as she held up yet another pair of spangled reindeer socks. "Thank you," she told Mrs. Soames, but the whole time she was looking at Erica. "I'll be careful with them."

Erica came over and gave Molly a stiff hug. "Thanks for letting me stay at your house. I didn't take your socks, or ruin your play, either, but I did borrow one thing I want to give back."

She handed Molly a greenish lump. "I found this in that special box on your dresser, and I figured you kept it for good luck. I thought it would bring me luck the night of my ballet. But I guess it didn't work."

"My lucky rock?" Molly cried. "But it did work today, for my skit. Everything went perfectly."

Erica took off her costume bonnet and ran her fingers through her hair. As usual the bangs fell just right. "I guess it only works between real friends," she said. "Anyway I'm glad your skit went okay."

"Me, too," Molly answered. "What I can't figure out, though, is who did the Donald Duck voice that first time? When we got to that part today, I was terrified somebody was going to start squawking when we got to the line about the tin cups, but there were only some giggles."

Stevie shifted from foot to foot. "I saw who giggled today when you said the line. It's those two girls from Roaring Brook who come over to take that special math class you and Suzi are in. You know who I mean? They both have short hair like yours, that's why I thought it was — "

Erica flung back her bangs. "Ugh, I know who you mean, even though their hair isn't like mine or Suzi's. You mean Tiffany Roberts and that girl she always hangs out with, what's her name, Leigh Something-or-Other?"

Stevie looked a little embarrassed. "I'm sorry I thought you were the ones who wrecked Molly's rehearsal. It turned out to be those two girls, I guess."

Erica made a pickle face. "Those two Know-It-Alls!"

Laura, Stevie, Shana, and Molly didn't dare look at each other and just waved as Erica went off with her parents, all of them jabbering away about Erica's great deed.

The girls heard the assembly bell ring and headed for the exits to go to class. It wasn't until they were outside their classrooms that Stevie stopped everyone.

"Hey, don't you three guys think something's a little strange?"

Molly had no idea what Stevie was talking about. "Like what, Stevie?"

"Like the fact that you're going to class in your nightgowns?" Stevie said with a big laugh.

Laura, Shana, and Molly stood there like three characters who had wandered in off the prairie.

"Oh, yeah!" Molly cried as the girls went to the girls' room to change into their twentieth-century clothes.

"Oh, no!" she cried when she looked into a small plastic bag that was scrunched up in the costume bag. "My reindeer socks and my jingle-bell earrings! I've been looking for them all week, and they were here the whole time."

"A lump of coal in your stocking, Molly," Stevie joked.

"And an apology note to Erica," Laura said. "Come on, it's only fair."

133

"Even if she's a Know-It-All?" Molly squeaked.

"Even if she's a Know-It-All," Laura answered. "Here's your clipboard."

"Oh, all right," Molly said. She sat down on a chair in the corner of the girls' room and right then and there began to write:

Dear Erica,

I'll start at the end. Our play was great, so great Laura, Shana, and I almost went to class in our costumes! Now that I'm back to normal again, I wanted to thank you for saving my play and my life!

Everybody's always telling me how I get carried away. I guess that's why I thought you ruined the rehearsal that time and that you took my things when you didn't. (You were right. I'm not so neat. I found my jingle-bell earrings and my reindeer socks stuffed in the bottom of my costume bag.) Anyway, I'm sorry I thought you did those

134

things. Next time, I'll think twice or maybe a hundred and sixty-seven times before I get carried away.

I'm glad your mom is okay. I hope she brought you back a great present.

C U When the Snow Falls,

Molly

What happens when the Friends 4-Ever are asked to be junior bridesmaids in a wedding, and Stevie is miserable? *Read Friends 4-Ever #10,* YOURS 'TIL THE WEDDING RINGS.

APPLE PAPERBACKS

THE GYMNASTS™

by Elizabeth Levy

Available wherever you buy books, or use this order form.

- -

Scholastic Inc., P.O. Box 7502, 2931 East McCarty Street, Jefferson City, MO 65102

Please send me the books I have checked above. I am enclosing $_____ (please add $2.00 to cover shipping and handling). Send check or money order — no cash or C.O.D.s please.

Name _____

Address _____

City _____ State/Zip _____

Please allow four to six weeks for delivery. Offer good in the U.S. only. Sorry, mail orders are not available to residents of Canada. Prices subject to change.

GYM1090